# MEN BEHIND THE
## MONSTROUS RAGE

# MEN BEHIND THE MONSTROUS RAGE

Alexei W.M Tan

authorHOUSE®

*AuthorHouse*™
*1663 Liberty Drive*
*Bloomington, IN 47403*
*www.authorhouse.com*
*Phone: 1-800-839-8640*

*Published by AuthorHouse    08/23/2012*

*ISBN: 978-1-4670-0075-8 (sc)*
*ISBN: 978-1-4670-0076-5 (e)*

# CONTENTS

# A CKNOWLEDGEMENT

I wrote this book from my point of view, would introduce some subject of Buddha's teachings by Theravadin elders that could more or less feed the mind of the readers about the logic behind. I blend these teachings into some legends of Werewolves, Vampires and Zombies due to the boom of popularity around the late 2010 and that I could adapt it in my novel as an establishment for the observation to the readers.

I've learnt a lot from various masters who had guided me to be a discipline disciple and also projecting the self esteem in me. Venerable Aggacitta Bikkhu as one and his assistant, Venerable Kumara Bikkhu taught me of how to access the confidence in me to face the challenges in the world today.

Dr. Ong Tien Kwan taught me of using the sciences to answer the happenings in the world today that helped me to eliminate my stress which is particularly helpful in writing the novel. He taught me of perseverance and patience to achieve something in my life that I really appreciated.

I also wish to thank Kevin Tan Shyh Aun and Valerie Tan Shuyin that are dedicated to become my supportive partners whilst I wrote this novel.

Besides, there are many masters whose words had become my companion that enlightened me into writing this novel. They are the Holiness Dalai Lama, Venerable Thanissaro Bikkhu, Venerable K.S. Dhammananda and many more that had advised me indirectly through their quotes.

Finally, I am very grateful with much of the effort given from Uncle Vijaya Samarawickarama who indirectly taught me of writing a playwright that had given me the idea of also writing a novel for the view of the world.

With further support from my godsister, Myriam Llyod Callachund as she helped me to realize my dream in publishing this book that I would like to thank her as well. It will also go to my fellow friends who had been advising me, Madam Ong Bok Kin, Mr. Lip Chee Wei, Tarryn Ashlee Fisher and Gulfaran Younis.

# EPISODE 1:
## THE STARTING OF AN ADVENTURE

I am always inspired by the stories told by my ol' man, Uncle Kringle; about the Dracula, the Wolves and the Undead as how they are formed and why were they become the icons for the horror movies. Sometimes I do wish to hunt them to show the heroic side of me. I also refer to him to know much about those monsters as sometimes I do think it's ridiculous to being so curious about their myth.

Uncle Kringle would tell me, 'It's good to be so imaginative but sometimes curiosity kills the cat.' I would carve a smile every time he ends with that quote. I know what he meant as many horror movies will show that way–men lost in somewhere, hearing something, follow the sound and lost one by one to the scary inhabitants.

Now I'm in my mid 20s and I have that opportunity to travel, travel as a Columnist. For two years I became an intern, my boss has given me a better opportunity and also the higher trust to do my own project. My major, to write about the Medieval and the Alamo, I have to do research for these two projects in two different worlds.

My first task is in the country of Romania. The country is so beautiful especially the capital, Bucharest. I could see the Cathedrals sculpted with monstrous figures called the Gargoyles. In some places, there are more effigies than the men. Some market place is still in the ancient manner, a market square with open air stalls all around.

The first thing in my mind now is to find a place to stay and my boss had actually placed me to a motel, Castel Hotel. When I reached, it was like 'Oh my god!' as that place is real medieval and is owned by a pair of Gypsies, believed to be originated from Bulgaria. The wallpaper is stripped almost entirely, and looked gross too. I can detect the gluey substance kinda like goo on the wall. Some place along the hallway too has its wall with scratch marks. The place looks as if it will fall in a week or too. The floor with cracks and creaking sound. The receptionist, erm, it looks like where is the counter for receptions? And next thing in my mind is why my boss did this to me!

I wish to find a better hotel but too hesitate as my fund is limited, so I think for a while as I sitting on an old stool at the corner of the so called 'Lobby'. A couple of a Chinese look alike came in about the 30s and ring a bell hung at the so called 'reception' and little while the older male Gypsy appeared.

'Ciao, you both have a nice pleasant vacation in this Castle!' he would greet. Then, the couple smile, fetch the keys and leave.

The guy doffs his hat to them then turned to me and smiles, 'Hey, you young guy! Plan to stay a day or two?'

'I'm thinking so. I think someone had booked for me a room for a few weeks.'

'Do I know the person? Name me please.'

'Yeah, Mr. Barry booked for me.'

'Wait a minute, I would check in my record book,' he nods and left to his . . . office.

Seems a bit funny as in this new world, technology should have mark its glory like most hotels would have a computer as stand by but this motel. Then, I think 'Oh well, ran by old couples and in such medieval place, there would be no surprise.'

Exactly one minute, he appears and greeted again, 'Hello, good afternoon. You must be Alex Chrimson and your employer; Gerd Barry did book this place for a week. Let's take this key for your Room 183 next block across the back alley.'

'I'm sorry . . . next block?'

'Yes, that is the luxurious suite complete with Wi-Fi facilities, anything you need son, anything you need. Also a great bar is served down there and if you need anything, it is managed by my son, Gerard. And enjoy your stay!'

'Thank you,' I nodded in confusion.

He doffs his hat as he did to other customers and I leave. As I walk there, 'Block across the back alley . . . Luxurious?'

When I reached there, it is stunningly awesome, as if a castle. It is unbelievable and the name Castel Hotel really suits that building. The block is 20 stories high and contains 24 rooms each storey and 3 penthouses at the top floor.

I walked to the entrance; there is a lobby–like an actual one unlike the old motel. Three beautiful receptionists are smiling at the customers and the supervisor is so handsome and pleasant. I actually registered there and the keys that old Gypsy gave are valid one for my hotel room, and it takes only a while to complete everything.

The baggage carrier greeted me for service but I declined because they are not heavy stuffs.

Thus, I move to the middle for the elevator and saw on my right is a club, a swimming club like an Olympic size swimming pool. I don't notice entirely the place is because I'm rushing to my room. I'm actually almost exhausted. While I was waiting, a hotel room service approaches; he is a tall black guy with tan skin and bald.

'Hey there, I'm Zirhoff, Dan Zirhoff.'

'Oh goodday! I'm Alex Chrimson.

'You're an Aussie?'

'Erm . . . How do you know that?

'Oh, written on your baggage sir . . . ♥ Australia.'

I laugh when he pointed that. 'Yeah, right. You are observant.'

And the elevator rings. We enter the elevator together. He is going to the 14th Floor while I am heading to 8th Floor.

'I am loving Australia. I am loving Sydney.'

'And where are you from?'

'I am from Brăila. My parents lost in Egypt during the treasure hunt.'

'I'm sorry . . . treasure hunt?'

'Yes treasure hunt. In El-Alamein for Great War military pieces.'

'Is there any news how did they lost?

'Some said plane crash and some said they are captured by some terrorists. But what I believe they are still alive in somewhere some tombs there.'

'But . . . but how'd you sure about that. How'd you know that?'

'Mr. Snikoff, my neighbor also was part of expedition. He was found alive and safely brought here. He said of something like zombies but many thought he's mad. Earlier I thought so but he mentioned that my parents are safe. I am becoming quite believed in his words and he's now staying in my apartment.'

'Oh . . . Zombies huh. I'm quite interested in that topic. Oh, I'm reaching my level. So see ya 'round!'

The elevator rings, the door opens and I step out moving towards my room, Room 183. I unpack my baggage and hang some belongings at a wardrobe. Also, I check around the luxury room–the bathroom and also the balcony. It is a splendid view when I 'sight seeing' the town through the balcony. Anyway, it is a long hour before the cloud turns dark. I'm not going anywhere and thus, I take out my Dell notebook and wireless network is detected. Truly to what the old Gypsy said, Wi-Fi provided. I start a sentence with 'As I reach Bucharest . . . 'but before I go on, a knock on the door and I open it. A handsome guy, standing 6 feet tall with a white blazer and he doffs his hat as soon as I'm in his view.

'Sir?' I asked with a little astound.

'Oh, good afternoon, Mr. Chrimson. As understood, I'm Gerard Rosicky, the manager.'

'Oh yes! Your father did tell me.'

'Right, I'm not going to be here for long . . . and here's the newspaper. I personally come here for a warning of not to open the door after 3 a.m. and apply this in case you want to really take a stroll. Anything else, please do call my extension number 05. Have a nice day.'

'But . . . '

Before I complete, he already left leaving the newspaper and a bottle of . . . crystal clear water? I'm wondering why such a warning is. I'm about to call his extension but later, I think it is best not to. I better refer to the housekeeper, Dan.

So, I continue to type my part for the column articles. However, all the mysterious thoughts started to haunt my brain. All sorts of weirdly figures playing in my mind. I close my notebook, thinking to myself that I might be too tired and wondered too much. It's good to have some sleep.

I thought I was sleeping for a while until my cell phone rings. I wake up to pick it and realized that it is already 2.58 a.m. My boss, right, in his time zone is actually afternoon.

'Hello. Alex. How's the project going on?'

'Man . . . Mr. Barry. Don't you know it is midnight here?'

'Oh yeah, I forgot. I want to tell you I have here, Ms. Saunders. You can call her Sarah. She is also interested in this project and asked if she might collaborate with you.

'Wait . . . what?'

'Night, Alex. Pick her from the airport tomorrow. She will call ya she arrived.'

He hangs up the cell phone before I even ask why. It's my nature not to have a partner even if the person is an expert to collaborate with me. I know I can handle everything.

As I sit there with no idea in my mind, I thought, why not I take a stroll as it is already 3.05 a.m. Despite the warning, Gerard said I can take a stroll with condition–to apply the 'lotion'.

I did as told, move out from my room, take an elevator to the lobby but to my surprise, the entrance is actually guarded by couple of policemen and also a few sentries. I thought maybe previous robbery might be the cause and so without any guilt in my mind, I walk to the entrance. One of the policemen stops, asking whether I applied the lotion provided.

Indeed, I nodded yes and they allow me to go out. One of sentries warn me not to venture into the forest. Now this is weird as why are so many rules to visit this country? Is this place infested with hooligans, and if such happens too I'm not afraid because I have actually learned Wushu in Hong Kong.

Okay, the town is nothing after midnight except a night club a few distances away from my hotel. Anyhow, it is too guarded by armed hooligans and punks. From outside, the Heavy Metal sound can be heard. An old beggar is lying awake in front of the club. I approach the beggar and throw in two dimes into his bowl, and then he stands up.

'A word of wisdom, son . . . ever wonder why the other places are guarded by troops and policia while this is from those youngsters?'

'No. Why?'

'You visitor. You don't know. The dead alive. This place is governed by those children. Policia would not interfere after 12. They are deadly, the dead alive fear to come near. So the government just let them be. Otherwise, the policia will already handle this area.'

'How resourceful.'

I'm trying to ignore him and am going to entering the club.

'Remember, young guy. This place, unpleasant. Devil. Don't follow their footstep . . . '

This time, I totally ignore him and enter the House of Fun.

' . . . when the time is right, you'll find your Master, sonny.'

I'm so shocked to find out there are several zombies' cages in the club. The cages are located at the both right and left side of the club. The bar is placed to the left right beside one of those cages. If I really count, there will be around 10 cages, 5 to right and remainder to the left. The performance stage is in front right where I got in from the entrance. The atmosphere is so unpleasant. The imprisoned zombies are hunger to catch anyone close to the cage but will be electrocuted if touches the bar. I noticed those zombies are actually displeased with the surrounding, the noise and the flashings. I am asking of how did the youngsters actually capture those monsters and no wonder, Gerard had actually warned me about this situation. And I refuse to enter. I did not actually step in and the entrance door is not actually shut yet but found out that the old beggar has gone! Now where's he?

Now what about the forest? It is located to the West, somewhere around the freeway. I've totally forgotten about 'curiosity kills the cat'. I am now filled with desire to actually bring myself into the jungle.

Few blocks from the club, a garage is still opened. A guy about his 50s is wiping his shotgun and that's all I can see through the window. He's still on even in the mid of the night? I inhale deeply then breathe out and approach the window.

'Hey, hello.'

'What? We are already closed. Nothing here. No more.'

'Just asking if you're still renting out unused car.'

'Yea. Tomorrow 9 a.m.'

'So what are you doing with all the lights on? Just wiping that gun?'

'What do you care, sonny? If you really want a car, you'll have it free, at the junkyard. If you really want to bug me, then I will have to plug a bullet to your brain. Now shut youshelf up and go.'

And so his warning says it all. I will have to find a junk car for a ride to the jungle.

About an hour walking through the town, I reached a junkyard almost nearing the freeway. Oh, the smell of bloody goat poo can be detected miles from here! I look around and found nobody so I decide to jump over the fence and if I can really get a car, ram through the gate and drive to the forest. As I climb halfway, a dog, a big German Shepherd run towards me barking in an angry and hungry look. I better not cross or I will end up devoured in his salivating mouth.

Then, from a distance, I heard a sound, growling-cum-burping type of sound. It seems like coming my way.

# EPISODE 2:
## THE LAND OF BLOODY HELL

The dog is retreating and after a few steps backward, it runs out from my sight. I slowly turn backwards and I can see a shadow of man walking like a drunken one. Looks like he is lost or something. Both arms are stretch forward as if a blind man is trying to feel something. When he is in my sight, it is a stunning figure as he is neither a human nor an animal but a zombie. An undead in front of my eyes!

Without hesitation, I climb over the fence as quickly as possible and ran across the junkyard. The zombie isn't chasing as there is no light or loud sound around. Even though I ran hastily but I manage to make only soft noise. Guess the junkyard are full of plastic craps and soft metal. Of course, those steps only produce soft noise. Next I realized is that the crystalline water is either a Holy Water or scent cover because I know that those Undead are really sensitive to the smell of blood and flesh.

After running for a while, I noticed a tower, maybe an abandoned scaffolding a distance away. It is still lighting. First, I think it is not wise to go there because those 'living dead' maybe prowling all over there but second thought, I may need some help there. Even if I think of tossing a coin, first I didn't have one and second, it is too dark to do so. Basically, eenie-minnie-miney-moe is actually playing in my head asking me to decide fast.

I eventually slow down and creep towards the scaffolding. Maybe I decided to climb up the place but as I moving nearer, under the dim flash of the moonlight, I could see something sticking out from the pile of garbage. I take a closer look and it's like fresh red paint covered stick, four branches still attached. The smell is however awful. It almost makes me puke!

I pull out the 'thing' and it appears to be a hand, fresh flesh of a human already decapitated! The ring finger had already lost. It started butterflies in my stomach and I am actually controlling myself from vomiting. It must have been devoured by the zombies. I also realized this junkyard is actually containing more dead humans yet to be discovered as I noticed that there are beheaded human head and bodies scattered everywhere. This makes me think it is better that I quickly find a car and get out of this hell. The first I need to do is to climb up the scaffolding to see if the tower has someone in, or maybe a phone to call to the cops.

I walk slowly towards the light and as I am almost nearer, it is actually true to my guessing—zombies are wandering all over the area. I am therefore forced to creep to the scaffolding and so I did, crawling stealthily passing through the zombies one after another and reached the place.

As I climb the ladder, I can sense how old the thing is. It is all rusty and if I were to climb up, it will make loud squeaking sound. But it's all depending on my luck if I can climb up in time. But later, I think it is wise to actually take a slower step as it will produce less impact to the old ladder. The first step only produces a small thumping sound to the ladder and I am relieved and so I climb slowly.

Almost the last step, the ladder already squeaks loudly as it is going to detach from the scaffolding. The zombies already alerted and now I'm furious—furious as how I'm going to come down and how should I defend myself against these zombies that are beginning to climb up the scaffolding.

I am getting nervous and I run quickly towards the tower. Inside, there is an axe in the emergency box near the window and there is a cordless radio. A table at the middle is almost decayed and most of the documents and papers are scattered everywhere. There is a rear door located behind a tilted shelf that actually looked like been rummage.

There's no choice for defense except for the axe. In a moment, the entrance is banged and scratched. The zombies have actually reached my hiding chamber and they are after me. It's unfortunate that the door is actually a wooden door. I'd better exit through the rear and quickly smash the shelf and the door with the only axe. It takes time for them to actually punch a hole to the wooden door and also I need time to shift the old shelf. I did it fast and so when they actually smash the wooden door, I had escaped through the rear across the scaffolding and down to another side of the junkyard. I need to only run a few yards passing the river to the freeway. But I determined to find a car so I could drive easily to the woods. I'm quite lucky at a moment to find a trashed car nearby. It is a Peugeot about 10 years old.

Quickly I break into the car and found out a key is still stuck in there. The environment inside is also awful just similar to the junkyard. Like many said, the luck is just a moment because it is impossible to start the engine whereas the zombies are approaching. I have to try again and again and the rumbles of the engine actually attracted more. My heart is pounding heavily this time.

Almost giving up, a miracle comes as the engine finally starts and I step on the accelerator as hard as I can to ram through the horde of zombies. Some that managed to climb the hood were flung to the ground when I accelerate and later, knock through the entrance bar and escaped the bloody place.

The sun is almost rising as I'm nearing the woods. Now, I remember that I completely forgot about the appointment with Dr. Jizrahk, a Historian who researched about the medieval era. The appointment is at 10 a.m. and my watch shows 6 a.m. I need to drive back and only able to sleep for two hours. How about changing and washing myself and to drive to his office? So as calculated, I can only nap for half an hour.

Due to the rising sun, there maybe nothing in the forest right now. I think it is best I clean myself and right away meet Dr. Jizrahk.

As soon as I reach the hotel, the people are staring at my car surprisingly. Some even feels like throwing up. I can't doubt much because maybe due to my dirty look. As I'm taking a turn, I look through the mirror and got a shock to see two corpses most probably a couple were sitting at the back seat. The girl probably is in her 20s and a headless guy. The girl lost her right arm and leg and the guy has scratches and bite marks. It seems that they are having serious struggle and in my mind, the culprit should be the Undead.

I do an emergency brake to make them lean to the front. I just hope nobody calls the police. Nearing the hotel, I stop in front of a cafe, Art.hot. Cafenea Vilă and look for Dan. I know he would be waiting at the valet hopefully to help out some tourists every morning. My guess is right; he is there about to attend to a customer as a jockey.

I whistle to him in a distance so that no one will notice me in such an untidy state. At first he never realizes but after I blew for twice or thrice then he turns around. Seeing me behind a fountain, he approaches.

'Damn! What are you drinking, man?'

'This is a long story, I will tell ya later. What do you know about the junkyard?'

'Haven't you read the newspaper given to you?'

'Yea. I kinda overslept. I don't have time for this but please tell me, what do you know about that place.'

'Aye . . . that place's infected. You're trash master you will never run your errands there. You find somewhere else.'

'Infected like what?'

'I heard but we locals are forbid to hang around there but I heard . . . Living Dead are revived there.'

'Gee hell . . . you see that Peugeot there. I've got it over there.'

'I'm not talking to you. You got that wheels, you're convicted. And better go clean up yourself. You smell rotten meat from up close.'

'I want info, buddy . . . '

'Alright, a week ago a couple died in that Peugeot. The same plate number. Now no more, okay? Trash that car if you don't want to end up in the cell.'

He left. I have to sneak into my hotel room that morning and because it is still early, none does notice me sneaking in. I throw myself on the bed. The alarm clock on the bedside cupboard on my right shows 7.44 a.m. In my mind, there's reflection of the zombies and then, my mind juggles of how to dispose the trashed wheels.

I bet the town recognized me of driving that car here and the worst thing is two corpses are at rear seat. The car is parked outside a café and at any minute, someone will open the café and may find out about the vehicle. The police will eventually trace me out with the help of the locals. And if I were to shift the car out of sight, it will ruin my shirt after bathe and next question–How would I attend the interview? Time is running up!

Suddenly my cell phone rings.

'Dude, you're really entering the hornet's nest are you?

'What are you talking about? Who are you?

'Me is not important. What you want now is someone to trash that Peugeot, dontcha?

'You tell me who you are, how you get my phone number and how'd you know I'm in trouble right now.'

'Right. Gimme 5000 leu to handle everything.'

'What? This is ridiculous . . . '

'Are you or are you not? Remember . . . time to meet your Historian. Let me run the errands and everything will be fine. Don't ask much and pass the money to the beggar you saw last night.'

He hangs the phone. Good Christ, someone's blackmailing me now. Yes or no, I have to give 5000 leu to get things going. After bathing, I approach the beggar asking him to meet me where we met and I caught a cab. When the cab passes by the café, the broken Peugeot is no more over there. Must be the man behind the phone did it.

As I am reaching to the meet with Dr. Jizrahk, Sarah Saunders called as she is reaching in two to three hours. Damn, a real busy day for me!

Eventually, I interviewed Dr. Jizrahk for about an hour and lots of good information on Medieval has actually obtained. If there's more of the Romania that I wanted to know, I really got them and I'm so appreciate with his kindness. Therefore, for return of his kindness, I wish to buy him some drinks but after a few persuasions, he agrees.

'Thank you, doc for your time.'

'I do much of what I can to help your project, son. I'm old now and if I'm not philanthropic, I think I can never do much any sooner.'

'I like the information about Vlad you told me. Quite notorious huh.'

'Vlad, yep. Many believed his corpse has actually gone. I personally believe that too. I was once the expedition to reveal the true him and when I dug out his sarcophagus, the corpse wasn't there.'

'Living Dead?'

'Why son? You saw them?'

'Actually . . . urm, no . . . I don't believe those. Ha-ha.'

'3 a.m. That's the time. Even now they are still wandering but not as dispersed during the night.'

'I heard 'bout the news past two weeks. Someone said to lost in the woods. Do you mean not dispersed as they are living in the woods?'

'I . . . it's better not to discuss this. Local authorities are actually investigating on this. Right, I have another lecture and I need to go. Thanks for the coffee.'

I thanked him again and he drove off. Now, my job is to meeting that Ms. Saunders at the airport.

Two hours drive across the freeway, I finally reached the airport, Băneasa. I held the placard as I reached the check-in point awaiting Ms. Saunders. Not long later, she appears few minutes after the plane landed. She spotted me holding the placard and approaches me.

She stood there, so gorgeous, so pretty. A long-haired brunette standing 5'9 wearing a white blouse and high heels appeared in front of me. I am stunned by her gorgeous look.

'Hi, Mr. Chrimson. I'm assigned . . . '

'Hi, Ms. Saunders. Just call me Alex and I knew you're my partner in this column. Nice to meet you.'

'Oh well, if everything is fine, why not we move. Besides, I'm already hungry now.'

'Of course . . . come along.'

We could catch a taxi in front of the airport and we head to the town. As we are passing the woods along the freeway, I notice something moves among the pine trees, something hairy and stood about 7 feet. It is black in color and something like a gorilla but this couldn't be because gorilla would not live here.

Maybe my imagination interrupts me. Sarah asks me what did I see and why do I look astound. I just shook my head.

Then she enquires, 'How was the appointment with Mr. Jizrahk going on?'

'You mean the doc. I've got a lot of information you can't imagine.'

'Wow, then I should work harder. I have only three weeks left to meet the deadline.'

'Hey, Sarah. We work in team remember.'

'He-he. You're right.'

The taxi arrived at the café, Art.hot. Cafenea Vilǎ and we dine there. Soon, I saw the old beggar I met yesterday. He was sitting in front of the theater just right opposite of this café. Soon, three young teenagers with tattoos on their arms and one of them wear singlet looks like demanding something from the old beggar. The old beggar looks like ignoring them, grabs his old broomstick and keeps sweeping.

Exasperated by his action, the youngsters beat him up and snatch the money in his container and run away. Furious by the scene, I ask Sarah to wait up and I rush to the beggar. As I almost get out from the café, the old beggar has gone.

I am surprised with what I see and walk back to my dining table. Sarah too was surprised and asked me what had happened.

I only reply 'Something keeps bugging me. Too restless I guessed.'

After the meal, we walk back to the hotel. She registers herself for the room our boss booked.

'My room is 245. I'm really tired now. Tonight I will call you for discussion okay?'

'Kay . . . see ya, Sarah.'

# EPISODE 3:
## TO BLOW AWAY MYSTERIES

Sometimes I can't understand why in this world, there's a lot of secret. Sometimes to reveal isn't an easy task. Life is always that difficult because almost everyday we're busy. Busy to collect data, busy cracking mysteries and busy to solve questions.

I just sit on my bed, TV on all evening trying to think what did I see last night and that afternoon. Who is the old beggar, who called to threaten me and what is the black creature I've just seen?

I determined to investigate on those, so I grab my camera and rush down to the garage opposite to the club. I've completely forgot about appointment with Sarah. The garage indeed is still opening as it is only 6.53 p.m. I couldn't be late again or I will leave with no wheels.

'Ah, it's you again. You're lucky this time I have the last one car, that second hand Prius to be rented out and it costs only 620 leu per week.

'I couldn't deny anymore.'

I paid him the deposit for one week and grab the wheels and speed off to the forest.

'Hey! Watch out how you drive! I don't want any scratches!' he shouts.

Sarah calls but I forgot to bring along my cellular. She calls for three to four times before finally giving up. She's also a little displeased. Whereas I'm in the woods for 'monster-hunting' to find out what is really going on with that big dark hairy creature.

I arrived at 8 p.m. sharp. A few steps from where I parked my car, I could hear growling of a creature. The growling isn't so loud and it sounds hungry, insatiable kind of hunger.

I try to find the source of the sound and move a little closer. The sound comes from somewhere nearer to the fallen pine trees. I build up a little courage to find out what is underneath and to my surprise; a Wolfman is trapped under a fallen tree. It is too feeble to push himself up and too weak to even move or break the heavy trunk. The scene looks like after a battle as scratches are seen everywhere. When he sees me, he breathes even faster as if he sees an enemy.

I am about to leave the place and leave him to die there but soon, more howling could be heard. Fearing to taking another step, I think that wolf may be useful for it owes me something for letting him free. However, second thought, I will only risk my life for helping him. Then, both kindness and ignorance comes juggling in my mind and only me could decide seriously.

Then I think kindness may pay off and so I approach it.

'You little beast, I free you this time and you owe me. If my flesh is devoured by you or any beast here, I'm sure you wouldn't find another intelligence next time.'

The wolf growls softly.

'I take that you promised me.'

It is a pact that my life wouldn't be endangered by any beasts in this forest. So I searched in the car if there are any useful items. In the trunk, I could find lots of metals like the toolbox, a rescue axe, rope and chain and even a saw. I take the saw and the axe thinking maybe the combo should be useful. A chain too may help sometimes.

I quickly chop the trunk with the axe. It is tiring as the trunk is huge, about 30 inches in diameter. I have to ax that trunk for 15 minutes before the axe could hack to the middle. I ask him to use a little strength to move the trunk. It seems to understand me and try to push itself up.

'Excellent, buddy. Excellent.'

This time I chain one end to the tree trunk, nearing the root and another to the trunk of the car. I start the engine and slowly drive forward to make the tree trunk to move. It actually works and the werewolf uses his strength to remove the remainder of that trunk.

It stands up looking angrily at me and takes a few steps towards me.

'Hey be cool. Remember your promise.'

Then, he shrinks. The fur turns into a man's skin and slowly it transforms into a man. I'm really impressed by his quick transformation but however he's still a tall guy. I'm only his shoulder level. He's hefty muscular man and having thin blonde hair.

'Who are you, guy?'

'Alex . . . Chrimson.'

'You shouldn't be here. Any mistake you will end up being a dinner.'

'I think I should go.'

'Wait. What are you really trying to dig up here?'

'No sir . . . '

'That's not a valid answer. Nobody comes here for nothing. You're finding 'bout us ya?'

'Actually . . . erm . . . I've gotta go. Nice day, sir.'

'Beware your answer. Running errands here is not a wise way.'

He howls and three werewolves approach from the mist.

'Now you're telling your pack. I freed you and that's how you pay back?' I warn.

'No. We fight together and we're the leaders of the rest.'

He signaled his friends to devolve.

'Now meet them. Nick, Peter and Nikolay and for me myself, I am Rowan.'

As I am about to shake hand with them, Rowan shoves me.

'We wolves of pride won't do that.'

Then, a voice from a distance appears. A lady's voice.

'Look like you're still long live, creature.'

Rowan quickly transforms into a Werewolf and roars loudly. Nick signals me to hide in my car and so I did. Peter and Nikolay too transform into Werewolf. In a moment three ladies appear. They actually appear by flying from misty scenery quite a distance from the woods.

'Hah, bloody dinner for me. And if you three are not going to stop me from taking him, then you will walk away unharmed.'

Rowan roars at her. He looks like readily to attack if she makes another move. She grows her fangs and so the others. She turns to a really pale woman and her finger nails grow about an inch. She flies towards Rowan and scratches his chest violently. The others screech at the trio.

I won't just stand here and so I grab the axe and interrupt the fight between Rowan and the Vampire. I hurl the axe at the Vampire. Then, she stares at me furiously.

'You are ready to look for hell!' she yells.

Rowan catches her and roars. He makes her totally immobile. One of her companion jumps to me at my back and readily to scratch me. Nikolay leaps to her and quickly catches her hand and throw her to a tree. Peter and Nick come to protect me.

I wake up and quickly get the rope from the trunk. As I did that, a Vampire grabs my shoulder ready to break me. This time not to wait longer, I grab her arm and twist. She's thrown to the ground. That's my Wushu skill. Again I bend her arm to the back and lock her to the ground. With the rope in my hand, I tie her both arms and make a deadlock. There, I held her captive right now meanwhile the others are still fighting.

'Stop now and look here!' I shout.

'What are you going to do with her, handsome?' the 'leading Vampire' purrs.

'War won't solve anything.'

'What should we do to release her?'

'Do nothing.'

'That simple?'

'Yes, stop arguing!'

Everyone releases themselves. So I release the Vampire too.

'Now listen to me guys. Who are you three?'

'Felicia. They are Lita and Kat in your hands.'

'Kay, Felicia, Kat whatever, why do you go against these wolves?'

'You don't call us wolves, genius. Only our clan can do that,' Rowan interrupts, already turned to man.

'Guess you'll never know our feud.'

'This is why I'm trying to find out. It's not in front of a big screen, Twilight or Underworld. It is real now!'

'Young guy, our battle is not your business. Now consider this, her release is our debt. You go now and never come back here again or I will never guarantee you will be killed by me.'

'I want to help and that's the purpose I'm here . . . I am . . . here . . . I guess.'

'Christ, you're too stubborn . . . '

'You believe in Christ, Jesus?' Nikolay confused.

'Oops . . . I mean Chris . . . Topher. Now you get off . . . '

'No! Not until I find out the truth.'

Felicia shakes her head and look to the others. The others shrug and then she turns to Rowan. Rowan shakes his head too and explains.

'I . . . don't really know. It's been a feud for centuries and if I have a chance, I really want to know the truth.'

'Me too, hun. I hope somebody will actually help us, the Vampire race to find out,' Lita sighs.

'So aren't you tired with this fight? For so long?' I ask.

'Actually we are. But she never stops,' Nick accuses.

'But you're terrorizing my territory,' Kat defends.

'Stop there you two. What is the meaning of territory? And especially, what with the zombies?' I question.

'What is zombie? Something edible?' Nick asks.

'Living dead . . . like us. There'll be something fishy going on,' Lita suspects.

'What I wanna do is to find out 'bout that zombie and then your origin. Got that? Promise me to stop hurting people especially me! You'll get the reward later,' I ensure.

'I vow so,' Felicia agrees.

'So are we,' the Werewolves vow.

'Well, it seems so late now and oh my gosh! It's 1 in the dawn now. I need to go.'

I grab the wheels and speed off to my hotel. Just before I sleep, I check my cell phone and astonished to find out there are 12 missed calls. Of those 12, only two different numbers and one is 'Unknown Caller'. Now I remembered I promised Sarah, but who will be the 'Unknown Caller'?

I'm too lazy to recall who'd I promised to meet and after shower, I jump to my bed. I'm fast asleep but after a while, I dreamt. This is horrible as someone is calling for 5000 leu in my dream. Later, figures of zombies haunting and slashing me and I wake up all out of this sudden nightmare.

Cold sweat all over my face. I'm breathing heavily. My heart is pounding fast. Is it the promise I broke to actually pay the 5000 leu is just an instinct in my mind or something in the hotel is really haunting me? The clock only shows 3.31 a.m. means I'm only asleep for 15 minutes.

The cell phone rings again and I pick up.

'Hello?'

'The ol' beggar is still waiting. Do now or suffer the consequences.'

I hang up throw the phone to the bed and walk to the balcony. It is a silent night outside and drizzling. Nobody is hanging outside except for some teenagers and wanderers. They walk around aimlessly. Troopers and policemen are chit chatting while on their duty for the curfew period.

Suddenly, a soft breeze blows some branches on the tree and when it calm down, the old beggar is standing below the tree looking at me. I quickly grab my robe and rush to him down there.

'Who? Tell me, who'd threatened me?'

'I don't know. I got this from him too.'

'A note? "PAY ME 5K LEU" and who the hell is that?'

'A boy gave this to me. I didn't see his face.'

'Who's that boy?'

'I don't know. But he's a Japanese tourist.'

'I give you this 5000 leu but remember, I 'll be watching you. I will catch that guy as soon as he comes to claim. Okay.'

'How?'

'You stay here. I am spying up there.'

As I turn around, the same cold breeze I felt at the balcony appears. So I turn around again and the old man has gone! I'm really stunned.

# EPISODE 4:
## TOMB RAIDING SQUAD I

I'm standing there like a statue. My mind is blackout. I'm not thinking either, I'm just . . . frozen. Soon, two policemen approach.

'Hey, what are you doing here so early . . . midnight?'

I turn to him for a while and walk away. My hands and feet are trembling. My mouth quivers. I walk languidly into the hotel, pass the receptionist and into my room.

I sit on my bed, eyes bulging as if a possessed man. Then, the phone rings. I slowly reach for it and listen.

'Good Alex. You've done what you are obliged,' he greets.

'Who are you?'

'Not important. What is necessary to know is that the dream will not haunt you anymore.'

'What . . . '

He hangs up. I continue sitting there clueless. If he said I would not be haunted by the figures during my sleep, does he mean I would not? Maybe I should try to close my eyes now.

I slowly place my head on the pillow, slowly gaining consciousness of what I am doing. The fear in me has slowly disappeared. Due to weariness, I slowly close my eyes and inhales deeply and try to sleep. He's right. I sleep all night.

10 a.m. Sarah knocks my door. She is disillusioned. A bit unhappy of what had happened last night. And even this morning I already oversleep. The sun shone to my face so brightly. I squint and yawn and when I looked at the clock, I grow a little hectic, plus the knock at the door and my clothing that remain unchanged.

'I'm sorry. Please hold a bit,' I request.

'You'd better explain yourself as soon as you open this damn door.'

'Oh my god! Sarah!' I whisper then continue, 'Right! Right! I will.'

I grab my pajamas and quickly put on and open the door. She's in front with a rather angry looking face. Her eyes are glaring at me as if she will kill me anytime. I know she demands a real good explanation. Just to say my cell phone battery has worn out will not be a good reason.

'I lost 5000 leu,' I give a reason.

'Lost 5000 leu and couldn't pick up the phone?'

'I'm at the police station. I forgot . . .'

'Why should you lie to me, genius?'

'No, I promise you I'm not.'

'Right . . . I called you about 9 times. The first one at 7.45 p.m. and the last one at 10 p.m. Now for the 2 hours and a quarter, don't just give me the reason of police report.'

'Wow . . . math genius,' I whisper.

'Sorry?'

'No no. I really did. They want a lot of information and I tried to think of anything to make them investigate . . . in fact . . . it's not easy you know . . . to think who stole my money.'

'You don't even inform me. That makes you a real prick you know.'

'I'm sorry. I'm a prick, I'm buffoon. What about I spend you some breakfast besides I'm hungry and . . . you're hungry too . . . for waiting for me the whole night.'

'You'd better promise me you'll never do it again.'

'With my whole life.'

I grab my car keys. I walk to my car but she is waiting for a cab. There she looks surprisingly at me.

'Where are you going? Aren't we waiting for cabbie?'

'I rented a car last night.'

'What for? Haven't you lost your money?'

'Yeah, but for convenience I rented a car. Only 620 leu per week.'

'I see. It would be a bit faster too for police report right if you have a car?'

'Oh . . . after the report, I ease myself in a bar.'

'I'm going to . . . '

'I think it's better if we have breakfast now. We need to discuss our assignment remember?'

'Are you trying to hide something from me?'

'Yes . . . I mean a surprise. I'll show you.'

In the restaurant, I look outside the window. The old beggar is loitering in front of a Medical Center across the street. He stunned me when once he turned around, he could spot me looking at him. He nods at me and walks away. I'm getting suspicious about him.

The waitress approaches and waits for order. I ordered bologna and mocha while Sarah ordered spaghetti and cappuccino. Still unsatisfied, she voiced out.

'Honestly, tell me what were you up to last night.'

'Police report. Why?'

'I really can't believe you. You went to the club but I can't smell any liquor.'

'Going there doesn't mean I have to drink. I am not into liquor y'know?'

'Right. Show me what you've done.'

This is really uncomfortable as she is becoming bossy. I still obey, open up my laptop and show her the PDF for what I really did. In fact they're unedited copy and paste of Dr. Jizrahk's lecture.

'Good,' she nods. 'Good piece of crap!'

'Pardon?'

'If this is really your masterpiece, I think three weeks will be too quick.'

'What's the problem? Point out to me please.'

'I don't want to tell. You edit it then discuss with me. This is all for our conversation. Thank you for the treat.'

She grabs her handbag and walks away. I feel so displease now as she really crossed the border. I feel like no longer the leader for this project and she got really carried away with her temper. As it is still early, I wish to work on the project and I planned to visit the library.

On the way to my car, the phone rings.

'Hul-lo Alex,' my boss greets.

She really did complain to him, didn't she? But I answer the phone too.

'Yes, Mr. Boss. I know what is happening.'

'What is going on?'

'Sarah . . . right?'

'She's awesome, isn't she?'

'Awesome? Yeah awesome'

'Yeah, I'm calling you because it's been long, pal. So how's the progress?'

'Sir, see it's only four days I'm here. I've been working on it. You don't worry sir.'

'Alright. I need draft. Send it by . . . following day. Okay?'

'Absolutely sir.'

Looks like Sarah didn't complaint anything yet and now I've really got to cheer her out. But now what is important is to edit and improve my part. I will even bedazzle my assignment if I have to. It took several hours in the library to work on it and at the afternoon, I finally complete the first part. That too is done with the help of a book with so much value in it. I am really satisfied right now.

The clock shows it is 3 p.m. My cell phone hasn't ring yet and I think it is best if I pay Sarah a visit and show her my idea.

As soon as I'm in front of her room, I knock the door. She opens the door and when she sees me, her face turns gloomy. This really makes me feel guilty but however I should be a gentleman to cheer her up.

'Hi, Sarah. Look I'm so sorry and I don't mean to be an asshole.'

'No . . . apology accepted. It's my fault to be short tempered.'

'So everything's fine? Coz I'm here . . . my part to show you.'

Sarah started sobbing that makes me wonder. She hugs me and cries when I'm sitting by her side. I have to comfort her and ask her to tell me her problems.

'My boyfriend two-timed me as soon as I'm here.'

Wow, a relationship problem and that's never my forte. Since I'm here, I have be patient to comfort her. Then, she continues.

'He said I'm never good at anything. Not on the bed or even in the kitchen. All I'm good is stay in front of the screen to earn big bucks. He said even he could do that on a skateboard ride. Now he found someone perfect who could actually earn more than I am in the racing circuit unlike me covered in the cowardly blanket.'

'Wow, that's really hurting. Did you say anything?'

'He's right. I'm too timid.'

Oh, and that's the cause I've been scolded in that restaurant. To show her daring side of herself huh.

'What's his name?'

'Derek.'

'Call him and pass me the phone.'

'What?'

'Call Derek and pass me the phone.'

Sarah dialed and as soon as he picked up, Sarah passes to me.

'Yo Derek buddy.'

'Sarah? You sound rough.'

'Even though it's rough, it won't be rougher than you.'

'Sarah? Hello? I thought we're over.'

'It's over because first it's your uncouth behavior I won't tolerate and second you're the world worst thug I've ever known. A grade 'A' emptiness, like many said 'asshole'!'

'What the hell, biatch?'

'No, son of biatch you listen! This is not Sarah and if you think your new harlot would make a million bucks for you then you're wrong. It's because we're working on something worthier than her earnings. If you ever regret it, think it not. Go on with her and if she ever cheats on you, then good luck with it.'

'Hello, Sarah . . . hello . . . '

I hang up the phone and pass to Sarah. She turns her face to the balcony trying to control her laughter.

'I hope you're glad with that crap smearing words.'

'You're really an asshole . . . '

Then we laughed together. I'm glad I'd make her chill at last. We worked on the project so smoothly and in a mean time we finished two parts.

'Only the last part remaining before we can summarize, it's a good job. Thanks to you Alex.'

'Sure, you too are amazing. I'm so impressed, and it looks like my thought of working alone is wrong.'

'Hey, urm . . . I've ordered something special . . . if you wanna stay.'

'Yeah, sure. What's it?'

Then, someone knock on the door and Sarah gets it. A housekeeper comes serving some dishes to her room. Then Sarah pays her some tips and turns to me.

'Here's the Kebab Special and some wine. That's for our progress. Let's toss.'

'Yes, thanks and indeed for the progress.'

'Should we, urm, have a stroll after this meal?'

'It would be a pleasure. I want to try out your rented car too.'

'Great. At least we can look around Bucuresti.'

As promised after the meal, I take her for a ride around Bucharest and we're really having fun around the river Danube. We even enjoy the sunset and there she speaks.

'You know Alex, at the first sight, I know you're the man who do things right. It is really a big mistake to have embarrassed you in the restaurant this morning. I owe you an apology instead of you did.'

'Sarah, it's my fault too to never tell you the truth.'

'I don't understand.'

'It's very hesitating for me to say, and during the moody period of you, I think it's not a good explanation too. But now, if you do believe in me . . . hear me as a team.'

'Right. Say it.'

'Everyone has a dream and my dream to be a columnist is not only because I'm loving it as a career but I'm adventurous. And in this adventure, I love myth and what I've encountered were Zombies, Wolf men and Vampires. You can say you'll never believe it but I personally saw them.'

'Hehe. You're scaring me right.'

'Alright, you don't believe.'

'I believe . . . you're nutter. Ha-ha-ha!'

I shake my head and as I turn to her, Rowan and Felicia appear. Rowan is panting but Felicia remain as calm.

'What's the matter guys?' I asked.

'I found a tomb. Believing it does belong to my ancestor. I need your help to find out anything about our feud,' Rowan explains.

'Yeah, Nikolay notified me as soon as he found it. Together we come because I thought of you, Lex,' Felicia talks seductively.

'What tomb? How'd you know them? Lex?' Sarah asked in confusion.

'He's Rowan and she's Felicia. They're . . . what I've said . . . Wolfman and Vampire.'

'You think you can make me believe so easily. I ain't a kinderkid y'know!'

'And who's this cute girl huh?' Felicia asked.

'I am Sarah.'

'Well, Sarah there's no time to explain. I've got to go to see what's happening,' I interfere.

'Yeah, better get going, bro,' Rowan supports.

'Alex, you'd told me you'll never desert me and if any findings, we'll do it. Right?' Sarah asks for approval.

'Right, Sarah but if you'll never believe what I've told you, how am I going to help this time? Just believe me now and you'll see for yourself later who are they.'

Sarah nods and as I am about to enter the car, Felicia stops.

'What are you doing, bronco?'

'My car's here.'

'Yeah, I know. Wouldn't it be good if you follow us?'

'Like how?'

'Like this.'

Then, I realized we're at the location. Sarah too was surprised.

'Is this kinda magic or am I dreaming?' Sarah whispers.

'No, silly. I'm Vampire and I can teleport easily.'

'Now this is weird.'

'Yup, and this is how we travel easily between casket and your world.'

'But I thought the casket will open by itself.'

'What about the casket which is shut properly?'

Sarah raises her eyebrow and nods a little. Sometimes quite mysterious isn't it? Me, on the other hand is excavating the tomb while Rowan looks on. I turn to Rowan and ask for help. At first, he's a bit reluctant.

'I can't transform to wolf right now. I made a vow to you but not her,' he glares at Sarah.

'Trust me you won't cannibalize her. Felicia is protecting.'

'Okay.'

He changes himself into a Werewolf and starts digging. Every time he sees Sarah, he started salivating like he's never been eating for a week. Felicia has to always block his view. Sarah . . . she just stood there trembling while watching us. At times, I would be her placebo. I would sooth her of how 'friendly' they are. It goes on until he finally dig the tomb. It is empty, deep and dark underground tunnel. I ask Rowan to jump in first as he has sense of smell and he'll lead to what we're finding. Then I jump in followed by Sarah and Felicia. We crawl some distance until we saw two diverged route leading to two caves.

Rowan smells and he crawls to the right one. We follow but Sarah who's already a bit tired crawls slower and Felicia overtakes her. I'm totally dumbstruck and worry and my heart beats rapidly.

# EPISODE 5:
## TOMB RAIDING SQUAD II

I quickly turn to the incident point and dig up as quickly as possible. Rowan also helps me and so does Felicia with the help of grown nails. Although we're tirelessly doing it, it seems impossible because the quicksand is so deep and every time we dig, seems like dirt from elsewhere will replace. We gave up at last. Rowan sensed that there is a route somewhere accessible to the tunnel underneath the quicksand trap. I just pray she's okay.

Rowan crawls until one point that is dead end.

'It is dead end, my friend,' Felicia alerts.

Rowan does not answer but he places his ear to the wall. So I did too and I hear windy sound from within so I try to break the wall. But it's somewhat impossible to just use fist and needing some super strength or spell. Felicia instead uses her psychic and in a blink of eye, we're on the other side of the wall. I ask Felicia whether she can bring us straight to Sarah but she shakes her head. She needs to estimate the depth of the tunnel to enable teleportation. She added that if wrong estimation eventually will get someone killed or stuck in the earth.

The other side of the wall is like a wide open space and every steps we take produces echo. The place is dusty and plain and I can only see with the guidance of moonlight penetrated through the ground. It is really dark and I have to hold them to be able to crawl closely.

We crawl until Rowan senses a hollow. It appears like a slide that we have to slide down to somewhere deep inside.

'How should we do this?' I ask.

'We have to do it. Keep sliding until the end, then we'll see what to do,' Felicia proposes.

We slide down and it takes some time to really reach the end. It is a long hollow tunnel about 23 meters in depth. Surprisingly at the bottom, the chamber is still illuminating. The lights aren't extinguished as if someone has been taking care of it always. The wall all along has its drawing in some kind of Hebrew scripting. I'm not a Jew and I can't understand the meaning behind. As I walk along, I saw a drawing behind a hanging torch, a painting of Lycan. That's the end of the Hebrew writings and beginning of drawings of myth. The drawing depicts of several hunters surrounding the enraged Lycan.

Next drawing shows the loss of one hunter and gaining of another Lycan. It maybe means the cursing of the Werewolf.

I follow the drawing and getting each meaning of the cursing until I finally saw a triangle it is another part of drawing that is not linked to the first one. Beside the triangle, there's a row of men whose heart is being weigh by Anubis. Does it mean Werewolf has association with the Anubis?

Then I saw a drawing of a wolf against a crowned man. Besides them is a woman carrying a child with a face of eagle. In my analysis, if I'm not mistaken, the woman carrying the child should be Isis as she is watching the battle of her husband, Osiris and because she is holding the eagle-faced child Horus which she bore with Ra and the battle with Osiris is done with Seth, another jackal god of Egyptians. He is always known for being evil. And in this case, the Lycans should have origination with Seth. Seth is also known for his curse.

As I read further, Seth would curse his enemies before killing and after Anubis gauges their heart, would return them to the earth to left astray for them are not worthy to be in the underworld ruled by Osiris. Only treasures like silver and gold would break them from the curse. Silver and gold are glittering means purification and the wares are used to guide most Pharaohs to the Netherworld which is why to destroy the curse on Werewolves, silver bullets are used. As silver are less expensive than gold means silver are main choice to be used as bullet.

Now I know the mystery behind the Werewolves. I move further to see what's behind the ancestral of Lycans. It says, during the Ottoman Empire, some Werewolf curses are spread to ancient Byzantine. This curse is less known because incident of encountering them face to face is not reported. The victims are most likely to be carried away or maybe during the Crusade War, many dead men are war victims thus any loss or anybody killed by Werewolf are remain secret. Some of these creatures had traveled to Romania and under the ruling of Vlad III in the 13th Century; some of this men are impaled. Ergo, they put their anger on Vlad III and his descendants and vow to be vindictive. The vie with Vlad III who was later known to be Vampire is so terrible that they became insatiable hunger and thus, the innocent men are the one to suffer the consequences.

'Now, that's the problem. Your feud is because of revenge huh, Rowan?'

'I think it's our problem that causes this huh?' Felicia speaks.

'Well, never mind. Let's find Sarah. I'm quite worried now.'

On the way to finding Sarah, Felicia mumbles.

'It's all about the Wolfman. I wish to find my source too.'

'Isn't that all about you was written by Bram Stroker?' I turn to her and ask.

'I doubt that.'

I shake my head and continue. Our journey stop as we heard someone cries. The voice is heard from other side of the wall. When I knock on, it is all solid and it is impossible to teleport to the other side. Then, I murmur.

'There must be something to go through.'

'Maybe it's a maze, Lex,' Felicia predicts.

Like it or not we must follow the wall. The route appeared to be snaky. Every round we take, at some turning the voice appear to be loud and at some point the voice appear to be soft and at some distance, we couldn't hear anything. In this case, it's really frustrating. Even though the maze is only a one way but it seems we're traveling across the Great Wall. Felicia and Rowan are still moving energetically. Not even a word of complain is uttered from their mouth. Because of their spirit, I will therefore strengthen to find Sarah. I believe this maze wouldn't lead us to dead end.

Finally, after several twist and turn we could see Sarah. She is bound to an interrogation chair. Surrounding her are five small people wearing wolf furs with Viking helm except for a man who is bearded also wearing the Viking helm. His face is completely pale and his eyes are white. He stood only chest level of Sarah. He claims himself to be 'Loki', the father of Fenrir Wolves. He is seen interrogating Sarah.

'Now, young lady. What are you doing in the chamber of Tyr?'

Sarah is ignoring him. She is scared and she's breathing heavily.

'Answer me! The damned! WHAT ARE YOU DOING HERE?' he yells.

'I did nothing!' this time Sarah screams back.

'This is the chamber of Tyr, the guardian of my sons, the Fenrir Wolves and you the damned humans are already doing something terribly sorry, something really guilty to come in this place without permission. Should we let you go, or should we hand you over to Hel?'

'I fell into this pit and how should I know it's belonged to you?'

'Ha-ha. Very funny. Everyone can use reasons but reasons never protect the person. So, to me since you fall in my Valhalla, it gives me reason to sacrifice you to my sons.'

'You can't touch me. Somebody will save me soon.'

'WHO ELSE COME IN HERE?'

'Me,' I show up.

'CATCH HIM, MY SONS!' he orders the 'wolf suited men'.

Rowan jumps to my front and howls. The men stun as they saw him. 'Loki' too was horrified to find a Wolfman sides the humans so he shouts at Rowan.

'YOU BEAST OF DAMNATION! YOU LEAVE THE AESIR AND YOU GAVE UP DURING RAGNAROK. YOU BEFRIENDED WITH MY FOE AND NOW, YOU AGAINST ME?'

Rowan just growls at him and hurls every charging enemy. Me, on the other hand use my martial skill to defend myself. It is just like an arcade because these men are not strong and easily to be kicked out. One of the men hit Rowan on the back and Rowan bash him up. Rowan leaps on him and shows his teeth readily to devour his flesh but I stop him. The 'Loki' guy sees this in fear and orders the men to retreat. Then, I release Sarah and together we teleport back to the forest.

Everyone leaves unhurt. Rowan changes back to the human form. The time now is 10 p.m. The full moon hasn't appeared so I ask the permission to be teleported back to the town. Felicia did and Rowan thanks me for my kindness. I think Rowan already put his trust on me and Sarah, so did Felicia. We are ally now and I think it is quite nice to befriend with monsters.

As both of them leave, Sarah looks at me and speaks in a sweet little voice.

'I can't believe you at first and it's my mistake. I'm a fool instead.'

'I can't believe too at first. But now I do.'

'How'd you get to know them and they appear quite tame to your eyes.'

'A little philosophy could help . . . and by the way, being philanthropic wouldn't harm right?'

'Philanthropic and wisdom? I shoulda learn something from you. Why not you tell me how could you be 'team mate' to them?'

'He-he, that would be a long story.'

'C'mon tell me, you mean guy.'

I just smile and ask, 'Would you like a late night treat?'

'Aww, don't change topic you meanie.'

'How could I tell you with empty stomach? Besides you owe me twice.'

Sarah laughs and looks at me with passion. Her eyes glitters, so beautiful and she gets closer to me. I don't know why I felt like magnet force that pulls me closer. She kisses me on the lips and I breathe in the sweet scent of her lips. She makes me fell to her temptation, like a Siren singing. The song 'Hallelujah' keeps playing in my head, and the Cupid shoots multiple arrows to me. Is that what I called 'Love'?

When she releases, I can see her blushing despite that night, the dark street only assisted with dim streetlights. I can see that we're falling for each other.

We had a wonderful night, good jokes in the café and even nice experience sharing. She admits that the first time she has a good laughter and having really good time with me. She never felt that during the time with her boyfriend. She admits I totally change her life and she appreciates every enjoyable time we had together.

I walk her to her room after the treat and she thanks me for my time.

'I'm very thankful for all you did.'

'It's my pleasure, princess.'

'Ha-ha. What did you call me?'

'Princess. It's that a sin?'

'No. Whatever. Right, it's late now and I can see you're tired after some action flick. Guess I will see you tomorrow.'

'I will and don't forget there are few more segments to complete. And before I forget, Mr. Barry wants a draft on Thursday.'

'Of course, my dear.'

She kisses me again and waves. I wave back at her and leave to my room. The night is filled with magic. Magic during the day, magic during the rescuing time and also magic as I having a nice dream in my sleep. No more nightmarish night like previously.

Below the hotel, the old beggar looks up and shakes his head. Then, he smiles and murmurs.

'There is something one could never understand. Because of defilement we'll never believe what others said and the worst, we never even think of researching. Like Confucius said: One would only find his teacher when he time is right. So do belief, it will only be seen when one fully realizes the wisdom . . . like me.'

# EPISODE 6:
## THE SACRED MAN?

It's morning now. Having a night time sleep without any distraction is so relaxing. The sun shines in and the cheering birds playing about at the balcony. I squint and smile while awake sitting on the bed 'What a nice day!' I think it's good to build a positive thinking. Today, I've got to send a draft of the first and second part and proceed with the third part, the final of medieval in Romania. After that, I will summarize and build up my column.

What's in my mind first thing is to have a good aromatic coffee and that's when I think of Sarah, oh dearly Sarah. I pick up the phone and call her and she asks me to meet her in 30 minutes. Of course I will. I wish to see my beauty in the morning.

I pack up my laptop and camera and other things useful for the last part of my project. Straight up I went to meet Sarah. I knock on the door, she opens up and there she stood so amazingly. I was like 'Woah!' and awe at her beauty. She hasn't make up but that does not distinguish much upon her image. She's just splendid like the Aphrodite. Only thing she's not a redhead.

She looks at me with sparkling smiling face that makes my heart beat faster and asks, 'Anything to please your princess with nice morning treat?'

'Perhaps, some good coffee for the morning?'

'Nice one. You just guessed what I'm going to have.'

'Ha-ha. Coffee is a must for me to keep me going on.'

'Like fuel for the car?'

'Kinda like. My princess, come let's go.'

I drive her to the uptown. We must pass the junkyard to get to the uptown. And that morning, I did not see any living dead wandering. Maybe this is why many people never report of any encountering with these creatures. Or maybe I am just imagining. I am eager actually to find out who is in charge of this junkyard. Do the zombies could actually climb over the concrete and tall zinc fencing or at least they could break through the zinc.

Since I am with Sarah, it's good not to think too much about the monsters. As we reached the uptown of Bucharest, Sarah chooses a diner where Spanish foods are served. The diner, Café Pepe Rubinas is managed by a Spanish man and according to him; it was founded by his great grandfather. That too is the first time I got to know Sarah loves Spanish food. She likes tortilla-fries-sandwich. While we are having breakfast, I notice the old beggar is there too, across the street.

He is really scaring me and I've got to find out about him. I pretend to go to the washroom and while heading to the kitchen, I ask a worker to permit me to exit through the back door. She allows and I haste up across the street to meet up that old man.

'How do you follow me? I want a straight answer!'

'You're too immature to get my explanation.'

'No! You're terrifying me. Why are you bugging me?'

'I'm watching you from day one you step into Rumania, you know. You never realized.'

'Old man! Normally I'm respectful to anyone older than me but you. You are already getting into my nerve!'

'And that means you're going to land your fist on me?'

'If I have to. And if you refuse to tell me why!'

'Just do it! I will only tell the facts to my students.'

'How could you have a student by being a pauper?'

'Wealth is not shown on the outside. Wealth is shown from here,' he points out by knocking on my head.

I become so angry and I start to punch him. However, I'm surprised that even though his movement is gentle and slow but none of my punches land on his face. None even touches his skin. He's just too good to avoid every attack. Another thing is he never fights back and he's waiting for me to be feeble. I'm really amazed by his skills. Of every attack I did on him he will say as such 'Never to let your anger overcome you', 'The wind turned fierce could uproot a tree but why not you?' and 'Remember that gentle water could be dangerous sometimes as it would destroy the rocks'.

I finally zonked and sit down at the pavement panting. I look at him and question, 'Who are you actually?'

'A beggar from the outside, a sage from the inside.'

'Sage? Which sage are you and what are you doing here?'

'If you ever heard the Tibetan Monk . . . '

'Yes I am.'

'I was a student there. I traveled forth to India to strengthen my morality and spirituality and I came back protecting Tibet during invasion by China.'

'And so you're Hindu? Buddhist? Or Shaolin?'

'I assimilate all religion and only harvest benefits from it and yes I learned Shaolin because it is a martial arts higher than you learned. I'm doing this because my nature of non-violence but rather self defense and physical practice. Shaolin is not a religion.'

'Should I call you . . . master?'

'Should I take you as my student? You find out yourself.'

Meanwhile Sarah, who was waited in the diner for so long, comes out and saw us chatting at the pavement.

She comes closer and asks, 'Who's this guy?'

'I'm non existing person,' the beggar answers.

'Non existing person? Kidding me are you?'

'No. If you don't believe, it's good if you don't question,' he smiles cynically at her and walks away.

Sarah turns to me and asks, 'Who is he and why he's so weird?'

I didn't answer. Instead I just say, 'Finally I found my master.'

Sarah just raised her eyebrow and without further questioning, we head back to the downtown. We still have to complete the draft and send it by tomorrow. I however planned to send today and hopefully my boss will compliment for our hardship. Besides, we'll be heading to Texas, USA after the final touch on Romania. America! How am I going to train my martial skill if we're going to America?

While working on my draft, I cannot really pay attention because I'm thinking of him, my so-called master. Should I call my boss to bring forward the column on Alamo but if I do, it would be disaster for my press company. I don't dare to talk to Sarah about this because I must assume that everything is scheduled. I can't concentrate at my work and so I decide to take a walk at the garden.

When I get down to the garden, Sarah was already there. She is working and she seems so focused. At times, she would breathe in the freshness of the garden and every time she did that, she seems more energetic. I'm really impressed and so, not to distract her, I turn back. The old beggar is right in front of me when I turn back.

'Can't work well huh?'

'Why you're psychic or something?'

'That's the present of higher purification.'

'Is that the reason you don't get hurt after beaten by the boys past few days?'

'To get beaten is an easy thing but to fight back, that's the most difficult task.'

'Wha . . . ?'

'Young man, you will know this. Do your folks tell you that to give satisfaction is better than to receive?'

'And that is why I must get beaten?'

'No, ha-ha. That is why you must tolerate. Otherwise, if you're carrying the burden of pain, angst and desire, you can't work well.'

'Wow, you're really a man with wisdom.'

'I glad I'm really are. Now go, complete your work.'

I'm so relieved after hearing his advice. He is like penicillin to germs in my body, he is the pain-killer and he is my medicine. I really am looking forward to be his student but there's side of me that really hesitate to inquest.

Because I didn't carry any burden anymore, I work really fast on the draft and Sarah is so satisfied with our work and immediately I send it to my boss. He congrats me for the beauty of my findings and I'm quite happy with it. I suggest to Sarah that we can celebrate the 'praising' he gave and she agrees.

She suggests celebrating at the night club she noticed not far from the hotel. And the club was the first I entered where zombies are caged. I immediately stop her. I explain to her that the night club is not a pleasant place with reasons like 'hooligans used to fight outside' and 'woozy thugs terrorizing the area'. Now would she like to risk herself for such a place? I'm on the other hand care about her.

Instead I suggest strolling in the bucolic. I think it is good to have 'night picnic' and romantic explanations of constellations. At night, there will be absolutely nothing to disturb our precious moment. She likes my idea and I felt accomplished to getting her agreement and to eschew her from trouble with zombies.

Me and Sarah have only 3 hours to pack before it's really late. I have in my mind is to watch the sunset too. It is best to arrive there at 7 p.m. and the time needed to travel to the bucolic is an hour. Sarah is good in making sandwiches and Baked Meat Cakes. I'm not a good cook but I try my recipe of Pasta Roll. I've learned some recipe from Hong Kong too that is Fried Tofu (Fried Bean Curd) and might be smelly. I dislike the unpleasant smell but I love the taste and nutrition of that food. It may become a great surprise for Sarah.

After everything is done, we leave the town at 5.30 p.m. and travel to the countryside. The air is fresh and the sun is still shining brightly, almost setting. She unpacks her lunchbox and spread a cloth over the field. I help her to arrange the food and drinks and we unpack almost everything except the bean curd. She is wondering 'what is the surprise I wanted to show later' but I convince her that there's nothing inside.

We are having a good time here and she shows a sign of satisfaction. She praises my suggestions and she even nicknamed me the 'wedding planner' and 'event manager'. I just smile and it proves that the substitute for being in the night club is a good plan. Besides, I don't want her to be horrified by the attitude of the youngsters and the lock-up zombies.

She points at the packing I brought again and I have to admit I ain't a good cook and so the only treat for her is the bean curd. She feels awful about the smell and after I persuade her on the taste, she obeys. She begins liking the food and eats another three pieces. She would comment 'I would give an F for the smell but the taste is so much so different from the smell'.

After having the romantic night together, it's time to head back to our hotel. Tomorrow is the day we'll be working together for the final part of our column and summarization. All the way back, we passed the junkyard and I saw a group of men wreathing around something. Sarah did not notice. Something is really negative going on around.

'It must be zombies,' I speak softly.

'Sorry?' Sarah asks.

I turn to her and shake my head uttering the word 'Nothing'. Then, she notices the group of men pin on someone. Sarah wants to find out and her camera is ready. I instead try to stop her but she has already got down from the car. She shouts at them. I try to stop her but already too late. She's standing a few distances a head of me. The zombies of course alerted by the shouting and charge to her. She's dumbfounded by the appearance of the zombies and I have to pull her away.

We run towards the car but there are zombies too coming our way. Some have surrounded the car and it is no way to enter the car safely. We have to run towards the gate. There is no zombies yet have been wandering there. We run as fast as we could but too bad, Sarah tripped on something and fell. Luckily, she trips on a hand of a cop—a cop who was lost years ago as he was investigating on missing people. There's a revolver on the sheath and it is still functioning.

I pull Sarah up and fire two shots at two nearing zombies. Both are good headshots I did randomly and both the zombies fall to the ground. The gate is not so far ahead. Sarah is still showing zealously the will to escape from this hell. The revolver I found still contains three bullets. Only three for our chance to escape and thanks to Sarah for that.

But second thought, she's not to be blamed because she didn't know they are zombies. Nearing the gate, there is one very large zombie. He is tall like 7 feet and is fat. He is bearded all over but is bald. He is sniffing wildly all over the area and I can see through the moon's reflection, his eyeballs are white and blood is all over his face. He wears a Middle Age shirt like a smithy. His teeth are so sharp and strong and his arms are muscular. He may bash up everyone coming closer.

I ask Sarah to creep silently under the half opened gate and be calm despite the wild horde is reaching us. I watch her from the back. I grab a long rod from the ground ready to hit at any approaching zombies. She understands me and did as I said.

Even though the horde is screeching loudly, it didn't alert that giant zombie. Maybe he's get used to other zombies' screeching. The giant zombie is wandering aimlessly. I hoped that Sarah wouldn't touch that zombie who is coming closer to where Sarah was creeping through. I'm busy swinging the rod at the nearing zombies to keep them away. After Sarah crawled through, she keeps jabbing through the fence to keep the zombies away from me.

I slowly widen the gate and creep through. I did realize the giant zombie is nearer and I hope I wouldn't touch it. But it didn't turn as expected to be. My butt touches him accidentally. So, I have to haste up to run away from him and that zombie was alerted. That angry zombie of course chases us and also the horde. They are so strong they could destroy the gate and the fence.

The whole junkyard is still a wide area and we have to go through lot of barriers to escape those hungry zombies. I only hoping someone will rescue us. And in a blink of eye, someone is there to rescue us. He is wearing a quilted hood. The horde is attracted towards the person and in midst of the dark, I can't see anything. I'm still running away from the big zombie.

As the horde is nearing him, one by one is punched and kicked by him. When I turned around, I just have a glance that he did some kind of drunken Kung Fu. He shows so perfectly that he can avoid any scratches meanwhile each and every butt is kicked by him. Some of the zombies' heads are even smash by his bashes.

I think it will be unfair if I never help. I hand Sarah the gun to protect herself meanwhile I personally take down the big zombie. I start to have the feeling of confidence in me. I start with crouching and hook his leg and he fell with head down to the ground facing Sarah. Sarah fires two shots at his head but he's still 'breathing'.

I find some rod to beat up the fallen big zombie. Some among the horde is really attracted to the ass-kicking guy and the zombies split up. Some come charging at me. I have to swing the rod at them and hit two. Because the other end is sharp, it causes some the two zombies' to inflict serious wound at the abdomen. They are still active and need some serious decapitation on the head to make them lifeless.

I spear their heads while they are on the ground but more are coming. I need to protect Sarah too and the giant zombie is waking up. I do a backward jump and double dropkick on the giant zombie's head so he would fall back to the ground. I stomp on him while warding off the zombies. At times, I would stab him with the rod and at times the other zombies would scratch him. This made him real mad.

He strengthens himself and pushes himself up. Despite how much stomping I exert on him doesn't fail him. He flings everyone on him including me to the ground. The other zombies are scattered everywhere. I feel real aching when I drop to the ground.

The angry giant zombie charges at me and Sarah fires the last one bullet at him. He turns to Sarah now and it would be real bizarre if I never help out. However, I feel weak now and I need to defend myself from approaching zombies.

The man realized Sarah is in trouble, faster kills the other zombies and goes for Sarah's aide. He does a flying kick that gets right to his head but he never drops. He's so zealous that anything came close to him will be thrown. Everyone, even the own zombie gang. The man seems not afraid of him despite his size is twice that man. He's now changing his style to Tai Chi.

He focuses on the relations of Yin and Yang and eventually gathers the power on them. His breathe slows and he felt so calm. The enraged zombie charges to him and attacks first. The zombie claws on him but all are missed. The man's movement is just like the old beggar when I fought him before. He's slow but sure and despite every fast punches the zombie did, none hit that man.

As the zombie missed every attack on that man, he takes the advantage. He concentrates at the zombies head, clenches his fist and lands a light punch at the zombie's face. Then, he sticks his forefinger and the middle one of the right hand together and jabs on the shoulder, the both side of the chests and one at the tummy. The zombie miraculously drops on the knee. Then, he does a spinning back kick and the zombie's head automatically explodes. Impressively, he did everything without tiredness.

Me, on the other hand is almost fatigue fighting with the other zombies. When he saw such, he lends me a hand to 'exterminate' the rest while I protect Sarah. It only took him a while to finish them off and he is still energized after. I'm so impressed because I have to take half an hour fighting with the giant zombie and another half to defend Sarah and fight the horde.

He approaches us, 'I guess you guys are alright. I hope you don't sustain any wound.'

'Thank you, sir. Who are you? And I admire your moves.'

'To know me is nothing, but to know yourself is an achievement. We always meet and there's no reason you don't know me.'

After he said that, he left us. He walks through the misty area and slowly fades away. For what I guessed, despite he's wearing the face covered hood; I know he's the old man. I remember him by the voice and movement and his little humpback body. I also recall his nature of speaking wisdom.

Right now, what I'm gonna do is to find back my car. Go back home, I must have a sweet dream and relax myself and so does Sarah. She needs to eliminate her fear of the terrible scenario just now. About the beggar, I will find out later.

# EPISODE 7:
## A NEW ASSIGNMENT

I'm feeling like spiked up the next day. I don't feel like getting up from the bed. Sarah is knocking on the door and the sun is so bright, so intense that I barely see anything around me. I forgot to pull the curtain and the window is still ajar. It is already 12.13 p.m. afternoon and smooth gale blowing in.

Since Sarah kept knocking, I have to answer the door. She stood there smiling and seems like there is no sign of irritation on her. When asked how long she has been waiting and her answer is since morning 9 a.m. I felt a little ashamed for living in neverland but she understood my tiredness for fighting with the zombies. She never seems so fear anymore when mentioned about the zombies. By the way, her hands are holding a plate of sweet smelling savory pasta.

My stomach rubles as soon as I smelled that. She asks me to bath first instead and not to show some 'hungry ghosts' manner. Like it or not, I have to obey. While waiting, she starts her last part of the project by the intro. She also planned a date with a professor, Wilson. He was known for his research of medieval especially the Battle of Posada and the period during Ottoman suzerainty.

I have to meet someone too, Alizair Şachăe and she is well known for historical studies on medieval Europe and also discovery of artifacts which is important to prove her explanation on medieval and late medieval.

Her appointment is at 5 p.m. whereas mine is half an hour earlier. Since she knows how to drive, she will drop me first. I pack up all the stuffs for interview and Sarah's already in the car. She drops me in front of a hotel, The Flamingo Inn and drives away. Ms. Şachăe is already waiting at the lobby.

She invites me to a guess room, the Stalin Room and it is so sophisticated, so comfortable and a relaxing suite. The new environment gives me more opportunity to ask more questions and most of which I ask are good questions. She provides really relevant answers and also with data and images as proof. She also talked of her experience to discover artifacts.

She told about Basarab I and Mircea the Elder who are crucial as the topic for medieval especially opposition of Hungary, Poles and Ottoman. She later tells of Vlad but didn't cover the whole topic. Hers is exactly as told by Dr. Jizrahk but since her time is up to meeting another person so I let her go. I'm really satisfied for what I've got today as the Late Medieval has been covered completely.

Meanwhile Sarah's meeting with Wilson is in his office at the University of Bucharest. He lectures on the Battle of Posada and the coup on Charles I Anjou of Hungary. He talked of Louis I Anjou too but not so detailed of which the Romanians themselves are condemned. He goes further into the formation of Wallachia and Transylvania and also the problems with Romania and Hungary.

Sarah needs a little more information from the Google, and she proven her dedication on her project. She took a little bit longer so

I decide to dine first at a restaurant across the street. She calls as soon as Googled and retrieves much of the relevant information to guide her of completing her homework. Then, she rushes to meet me. She would be so hungry and I offer her my humble side to spend the evening meal. Part of it as a celebration for the promising information I've got from Ms. Şachăe. It is best that we combine our information and summarize accordingly. After finishing, we submit to Mr. Barry.

On the way back, Rowan appears. He races with the car I drove and I have to brake immediately I saw him. He's panting noisily and changes back to him human figure.

'What's the matter Rowan?'

'You've seen Nikolay, don't you? And Nick.'

'No I didn't.'

'Weird, they hunt for food in the jungle and I've heard their howling later east of this area.'

'Is it the junkyard?'

'Ah! I guessed. I saw your car so I wondered.'

'Shit! They are attacked by . . . '

'Zombies we stumbled yester night?' Sarah questions.

'They must be dead, the horde is large!'

Rowan quickly rushes to the junkyard. Me and Sarah followed too. As soon as we reach that ground, Rowan sniffs here and there and he sensed something strong not far from here. The smell of carcasses—fresh carcasses. Rowan then pulls up the cadaver. It is brownish furry and already half consumed. I'm shocked that it maybe Nikolay's body. It means they were fighting the horde of zombies before we arrived and that Sarah's interruption could have attracted them to us.

Rowan smells some more and not far is another fresh carcass. Mutilated fresh carcass with blood pool still damp. That must be Nick. When he pulls out the reddish fur cadaver, I already confirmed that is. I'm so sorry for what I saw. Rowan is disappointed too just he cannot show. He asks me to bury the bodies in a suitable location and with a little honor for the wolf warriors.

I carry their bodies to the ground near an abandoned convent. Rowan digs out two holes fast and I bury them. I preach words of elegy and epitome to make the rites more formal and Sarah sings some solemn songs. Rowan and Peter give their speech and as we end the ceremony, Peter quickly rushes from the area. I try to stop but was too late. He never listens and he disappears quickly.

Rowan thinks he is fighting the Ghoul Lord. I became a little furious at Rowan for why he isn't stopping Peter. According to Rowan then, a wolf must hunt in pack but if the hunting team fails because of one, then the only one must sacrifice himself to bring back grace and pride to them even though they are dead.

'But if we're team, we should fight along right?'

'Not as easy as you think, Alex. I can't stop him anymore and maybe he's dueling with the Ghoul Lord now.'

'Rowan. You maybe right he should fight alone but you're belonged to the pack. His problem is also yours.'

'Yes, I am but you're here and I'm the last wolf to protect you.'

Felicia, Kat and Lita later arrive.

'I'm so sorry to hear of their passing away. I hope there's something I could help out,' Felicia offers.

'Good, they need to fight the Ghoul Lord,' I mumble.

'Ghoul Lord? Isn't here but the America.'

'How'd you know that?'

'We're vampires, associated with the undead.'

'And so Peter is chasing for nothing?'

'Guess so . . . '

Rowan became enraged and shoves Felicia away.

'You don't talk of pride of undead! I knew it, you collaborate with the zombies!'

'No . . . what are you talking about?'

Rowan grew twice the size and changed to Werewolf, an angry one. He bashes up Felicia and Kat and Lita come for help. I was even thrown when nearer and Sarah is so afraid she couldn't do anything. For Rowan, Vampires and zombies are the same. The Undead! Rowan repeatedly punches Felicia on her face and scratches her back. She heals fast but every time she recovers, Rowan will wound her. Lita and Kat couldn't do anything but to mount on Rowan and slash him.

Rowan would hurl them everywhere and roars and also settle with them. Anyone who could stop him will be attacked. So I have to use the last resort, to use my immunity.

As Rowan is charging at Lita, I jump to his front and do a Reverse Bicycle Kick. The kick got right on the chin and he was thrown to the ground.

I jump on him and shout, 'Rowan stop being a wild boar! It's not their fault!'

Rowan ignored. He pushes me aside and continues charging at Lita. This time I quickly catch him and hook his leg. Instead I hurt myself because his leg is like a tree trunk, so tough. This time, Lita is unlucky. Rowan grabs her on her neck and scratches her stomach. Blood splashes everywhere but Lita is still healing. I take a big stone from the ground and knock Rowan on his head. He turns back at me, feeling dizzy and then he drops to the ground. All back to man.

Lita and Felicia are almost incapacitated but they recover fast. Kat wakes up and murmurs, 'This guy need an anesthetic shot, he's damn strong!'

Then, I speak, 'I need a place where he can calm himself. Right now, Peter is the crucial person.'

Lita and Felicia offer to find Peter and ask me to take a rest. I drive Sarah home and all the way I apologize. 'I think I bring up so much chaos to you. You encounter much brutality with me.'

'It's that the way you breaking up with me,' she asks jokingly.

'Of course not my dear. If I were to breaking up with you, I wouldn't do it in unsafe scenario.'

She laughs and kisses me on my cheek. She claims that I protected her so much and worth dying for. She also claims that she will make our love everlasting like my sacrifices to her.

When we reach the porch, Sarah notices the old beggar sitting by the fountain. The beggar is looking right to me and Sarah asks me to talk to him. So I approach him.

'Night, master. What are you doing in such late at night?'

'Perhaps destiny has spoken that there is nothing to fight evil except the person I'm fated to find.'

'Is that . . . what you meant . . . me? I'm the rightful person?'

'The chosen one will come to me, with two cups of tea and an offer of him to become my student.'

I am delighted to hear that and quickly call Sarah to prepare me two cups of tea for the 'student enrolment'. He smiles while sitting at the fountain.

Sarah comes down with the tray of two cups of tea and I kneel before him. He smiles again. Sarah then comes closer and I offer him a cup of tea. I myself get another cup and ask him to be my master. Then he preaches, 'Of a kingdom ruled by a king, the king must have an heir, the rightful heir for the throne. Like a master should have one rightful student to inherit the teachings. If I'm right then drink a little from your cup.

I drink a little.

Then, he continues, 'On the ground so many leaves but the number of the fresh ones none so many as the tree. Like a master would only teaches what is important to his student though the master is one of the resourceful. You agree then drink a little bit.'

So, I drink a little again.

He preaches the third, 'Like the mountain so high enough, but the cloud is higher. To question which one is higher gives infinite answer but why not just say what you see as the highest. Like a master teaches a student, the student should accept the master's teaching without asking which level is high. After all, they are benefiting to the student. If you accept then drink a little.'

And I drink a little.

Then he preaches the fourth, 'For a minter, he has to mine the copper ore and in order to do that, he have to do it patiently, without complain. Bringing forth the heavy load, he has to separate from dirt. In order to do, he does it patiently, without complain. Finish washing and separating, he has to refine. Doing so, he takes time and be patient, without complains. After refining, he has to mold and cool off to shape a coin. These processes are all needing patience and no complain. For every hard work you endure you promise to do with dedication and without complain then drink a bit from the cup.'

Then, I drink a little.

And the last preach, he says, 'Like a tiger, they are fierce and wild. Even such, they will not attack the villagers as they like and if it sees one, it will not show its claws. Only if there is such threat, will it attack or if it's hungry. As such, you vow not to show your pride of your skills and not showing off what you've learn. Only do it as a matter of helping, defending and exercising. Take the last vow and drink from the cup.'

So I finish the cup and he smiles. He mentions, 'Call me Luo-Fu' and he drinks from his cup.

I nod and quickly get up and say, 'Thank you, Master Luo'.

He smiles, 'Excellent, excellent'.

Then, I ask haltingly, 'Master, are . . . are you . . . the one . . . who . . . who saved . . . us?'

'Like I say, you're the destined I am everywhere you go. Yes, I saved you.'

I thank my master again and he reminds that the first training will be tomorrow afternoon. I just can't wait for the training day so I sleep early today. Sarah reminds me to call her during my training time.

Suddenly, Rowan roars at me. Zombies are surrounding me and someone I couldn't see of his face is sitting on the throne in front. Rowan seems furious with me and later, the zombies approach him and there they tear his flesh and the scene looks gore to me. I can't bear to look at his suffering. Rowan did fight but he alone couldn't overcome the large number of zombies. Felicia and Lita later arrive and they flew to the mystery guy. Nearing him, the guy chocks them.

He throws them to the zombies and they are first beheaded then their fleshes are torn by them too. The zombies are so hungry and they eat every bit of them. Kat who comes in late try to save me out but the guy noticed. The zombies are so preoccupied in tearing the victims' meat so the guy ordered someone to capture me. That 'Loki' guy we defeated before tripped me and the zombies come closer and slashing my back. I'm shaking here and there and . . .

I wake up. It's already 6 a.m. and it's still dark. I'm having nightmare! Master Luo is sitting beside me.

'You see them, did you?'

'What? Master Luo? How'd you come here?'

'You didn't lock your door, son. Time for training.'

'Ye . . . s. I guess Sarah wants to see too.'

I quickly clean myself and wakes Sarah up. Together we follow him to the countryside. He preaches, 'For all training, mind is an important thing. Like a central of the government, it rules the functions of our body. If the central government loses its confidence, so do the other state government. They die out slowly and like our mind. If our mind is crippled, then we can't move the rest of our body, our limbs. Then, we are paralyzed. So to train your body, first train your mind. We would meditate here.'

'Meditate? Like the 'Om . . . 'word coming out every time we breathing?'

'Not exactly. To meditate is to focus on the breathing and we need to be calm. If there are sound, we observe them and if there is chaos no matter is our mind or the external, we observe. If there's repulsion, we observe and if there's attraction, we observe. There's no need to fight yourself. Just take them as nature. So let's start.'

So I close my eyes and meditate but he didn't. He instead with eyes open, he walks around me. Sarah who was listening too tries to meditate but both of us didn't reach the state of calmness. My master I believe already calm himself down because when he closes his eyes and walks, he walks in the same circle, never did he felt dizzy and stray too far.

I breaths in and out but never feel or see anything. I just can't tolerate my tiredness and the bombardment of the mosquitoes. At times when I feel like slapping a mosquito, Master Luo will stop.

'Concern not about your pain, concern lot on your brain.'

I'm impressed. His eyes are close and meditating but he can read my mind. How'd he do it? His circle is quite big and quite far from me but anything I do, he's able to sense.

About an hour we meditate and he stops. 'Bring yourself back to Earth,' he tells. I just can't wait to come back to Earth. I feel nothing but images in my brain. I am tempted by any thoughts that haunted my mind. Master keeps telling not to care but observe but instead I was lured. Anyway, there's no thinking of quitting yet.

Master Luo then leads me to the hill.

'We both will jog to the mountain and back to here by 9 a.m. A long period for us to do so and a long meditation trip besides observing the colors of nature.'

'Uh, okay I guess.'

Sarah tells us to go while she's waiting below trying to crack the Master's very first teaching.

All the way up, he mentioned of such, when the mind is ready the body will always prepared for the extreme. This is how a king commands the government. For me, it simply means when I'm already meditated, the calmness will lead me to more physically exhausting activities. For all that are done, I'm still energized.

Until the middle of the mountain, I'm already a bit 'worn out' but Master jogs so naturally. Even though he sweated much but he is still calm for I am gasping for air and it seems impossible to return at 9 a.m.

Then, Master speaks, 'Why young man? Already struggling in the middle of the sea? If you can't swim to the side, then you'll be lost in the middle of the sea.'

'No, but how'd you maintain tranquility and stamina?'

'In every step we take, observe well. This is not sprinting, so no need to rush but see the beauty of your surrounding. If the nature speaks to you, greet back and you'll never wear out.'

'But you said we must be back at 9.'

'I said that but never emphasized. If you really jog and feel the nature, feel the surrounding well and see for yourself the relaxing side of everything, perhaps we'll be back at 8.30 a.m.'

I'm so admired with his patience and I try to follow his style of jogging. Miraculously, I did everything without tiredness and we reach the peak in a short period. He praises me for my concentration to the surrounding and advice me to be in that state while meditating.

# EPISODE 8:
## THE MIND GAME

Sarah is still waiting below and cracking the secret behind meditation. Me and Master Luo are on our way back down. We enjoy the scenery very much. He instead enjoying behind his silence. I'm thinking of asking something but too hesitate. I fear I would distract him if I did. He instead sensed something and without me questioning, he answers.

'If that's your question, I was a German, a Gestapo and also a notorious killer. I killed many innocent people only during war but not the Holocaust. I felt that that was really wrong as I can see the fear in their eyes. The dead, their fist clenched as if they will never let me go. I did only 2 years and 2 years in the battlefield is worst than the netherworld. So I followed Heinrich Harrier in his expedition to Tibet. We were caught by the Tibetans but I escaped. I was harbored in the temple and none of the Nationalists could detect me. I decide to become a monk then and there I learned Buddhism. During the China's invasion, I was held captive and taken to China where I should be beheaded but I learned somewhere in the mountain of Gui Lin, I could learn Shaolin and thus, I escaped forth to the temple.

I've learnt Shaolin for 6 years and achieved the Chief Monk in short time. I was the record breaker there. I heard that there's connection between Buddhism and Daoism but I must challenge Guang-tai from a nearby temple to protect our Shaolin monastery. Guang-tai was a great fighter and we fought for 3 days where the last day, we fought almost 6 hours when I used my final move to defeat him. Because he was impressed with my skills, he asked for diplomacy and we exchanged skills and that's how I learned Tai Chi, Qi Gong and many movements.

'How's Buddhism anyway?'

'Depends which Buddhism you're asking?'

'Huh?'

'If I were a Theravadin, then I'm not into martial arts. They believed to war is not by using strength but to use wisdom. If Mahayanese, like the Tibetan too, there will be assimilation with Dao. Anyway, these three Buddhism are as harmony like a tree bearing the leaves, the fruits and the roots.'

'It means you has the combination of these three Buddhism?'

'I did explore here and there to research for scriptures. Buddhism is not a religion but rather philosophy. To combine these three is nothing and to separate them is nothing. Like water, if you a cup, still water and if you add another cup, still water. Then, because they are harmony then there will be no war.'

'Why not religion?'

'Buddha enlightened because of his realization, not the help of the gods. If a religion then we'll believe god creates everything but not a Buddhist. If you set a fire, would the God descend to create it for you or you need the tools and your own energy to light up?'

'Wow, impressive throughout the explanations you gave.'

'I guessed I'm talking too much and we're nearing the bottom. Keep focusing.'

I nod to him. The time shows only 8.15 a.m. and we're already reaching the bottom and that's real awesome. I think I've learnt a lot from this Master and I will show my enthusiasm in his teachings. He could read minds, he could bring himself to the state of ultimate tranquility and also the master of martial arts. He can teleport too if I guessed right.

When we reached the bottom, Master Luo noticed that Sarah is still struggling, so he is kind enough to tell Sarah, 'The mind is running like a wild horse. If you can tame a wild horse, why not you tame your mind?'

Sarah smiles and looks up to him, 'How could I tame the wild horse if I don't have the apparatus?'

Master Luo then answer, 'How could you light a fire if you don't have the fire?'

'With the fire stone?'

'Yes, with the fire stone. Like your mind only be calm if you find the means to calm your mind that is by observation. Observe your breath, your posture and of course your thoughts. Don't let thoughts to disturb your mind. Rather be it reaches the peak and down to valley, it will fade and rise. Just see but not touch and this is how you relax when watching the nature. Our mind works like that.'

Sarah understands quick and she did the meditation process without distraction next and she easily tranquil herself. Master Luo then smiles, understands that she is ready for everything. Master Luo then turns to me, 'Would you be that easy?'

I bow to him and nod. Master Luo then nods to me as he will never fail to choose the rightful person. Mr. Luo then dismisses us and reminds me to prepare for tomorrow's training. He also reminds that the training will be a little tougher and mind challenging. I bow again and we leave him.

Sarah feels a little hungry and asks if we could have breakfast nearby. I agree and we find out that there's a Snack Bar. Though it's a Snack Bar, it looks like a hut, beautiful in the outside but empty in the inside. There's only few workers inside and the number is about six; a bartender, a waiter, two cooks, a cashier and a cleaner. We are greeted by the waiter as we entered the bar.

The waiter takes our order and so I take the opportunity to ask, 'Sir, I wonder why is it so empty like there's no customer at all?'

'We used to operate a long hour sometimes may go up to 23 hours. The staffs here were so many last time numbering about 28 of them working on shift and the customers also were so many that we'll be very busy. This bar was owned by three persons and now one of them became the cashier there.'

'You mean the cashier is the boss?' Sarah asks.

'Yes he is the one. But due to argument, two of them quit leaving him alone here. They ran their own bar too. One operated near the resort and another near to the downtown. However our business is still the best. We're central of attraction from the both sides and the business that affected the most is that bar near the resort. So the boss is envy with our success he decided to buy over our land. He would offer 600000 leu for the asset which is twice my boss' initial investment.'

'Then it is good if he sells right,' I whisper.

'Of course not. This land is his ancestor's and he developed the bar much from his effort. He loves this property very much. Being angry with his tough decision of not selling this land, the boss used harassing method like chasing out the customers and vandal as warning.'

'How long was this place being harassed?'

'About a month already they keep troubling us.'

I think if it's early right now then there would be no trouble so we order breakfast set that includes pancake and cappuccino. We enjoy the food and no doubt, it could attract more customers.

Later four guys enter the bar and their looks unpleasant. I sense something will go wrong but I eat calmly. So did Sarah. One of the guys noticed Sarah and he seems attracted to Sarah's beauty but Sarah is still eating peacefully trying to ignore his staring. But the guy, looking for trouble comes closer. My early guess of 'there would be no trouble' proven wrong as his hand is approaching Sarah.

I know that and faster grab his hand and twist and he moans in pain. So the other three guys come for his aide. With my left hand still twisting that guy's wrist, I whip two guys with a kick and bash another who comes to my right.

The person whom I twist his wrist is thrown outside then I order, 'If you're condemning yourself for being long life, let's settle outside.'

Those three thugs follow me. Outside the bar, they quickly surround me and walk in circle. I have to be observant if any of them make a first move, I should have shoved them away. So the first person start to attack is that of my back. I quickly do a spinning kick right to his face. Then, the person in front jumps to me but I kick his chest and he fells. Then the other two do a simultaneous attack but I evade and when there's a chance, I punch one of them on the face and another on his stomach.

As they move backwards a bit groaning in pain, I put a powerful reverse jumping kick on both of them and they too hurled further to the ground. The guy I earlier beat up then grabs my back and tries to bear hug me. He raises me high from the ground and another one charges at me but I have him kicked with my own two legs and butthead the guy who grabs me. Then I elbow his chest twice before finally knee him. All of them lying on the ground aching here and there and so I hand them over to the cops. The inspector praises me for bravery and he promises to watch over the bar over certain period until the peace is restored.

The owner o the bar thanked me and as gratitude, he wouldn't charge my breakfast set. Me instead, feels awkward with that offer paid him since he is running a business.

Sarah is so happy with my kindness and also saving her from being assaulted again. She thinks to learn martial art indeed is another advantage like me could defend myself is any trouble arises.

I suggest to her to refer to Master Luo if she's interested to learn. She really did refer to him when we arrive at the hotel and she noticed him. Master Luo at first feels a little hesitate for she is a lady and he never trained any woman before. But after persuasion, Master Luo thinks she has the right to learn as she will be faced with dangers. Master Luo agrees but he will need to facilitate everything needed for training for a woman. If successful, we'll be training together tomorrow. Sarah is indeed joyful to hear that.

Just as we are back our room, Sarah starts meditating. I check for flight ticket to USA for next week. I believe we will cover the topic on Alamo in a week since the synergy of both of us could do thing efficiently. The only available hour will be 8 p.m. at the Bucharest Airport, the Otopeni.

I call Sarah for reservation but I can't get through. She activates the voice mail because she needs concentration for the whole half an hour meditation process.

Because I couldn't get through her, so I'm a bit worry and I go over to her room. When I knocked, there's no answer, so I call again. Nobody managed to answer my call. So many times I knock but no one answers. I rush to the garden to see if she's there but no. I become more nervous but after her meditation, she checks her phone and she's shocked to find out 13 missed calls all by me.

She quickly contacts me and apologizes and that's how I relieved. She also agreed to book the only ticket to USA. At night, we have dinner at an exquisite restaurant we order the local delicacies. She describes of how peaceful she was during the meditation and that I should try. I think she's really into spiritual development and I'm proud of that.

Before we go to sleep, Sarah asks if she can move to my room and I'm stunned with that. I'm speechless for a while and when she asks again, I just utter 'as you wish'. The question, 'Is that the next move of our relationship?'

Her reason 'So I won't be worried if she never picks up the call'. I laugh at her statement. Indeed a good idea. Indeed she really falls for me. She moves in the very next morning even before Master Luo 'sneaks' in to my room. I think I should just double the security in case of intimacy and a sacred man sneaks in and saw everything. Isn't it a bit rude?

However this morning, he knocks on the door. Me and Sarah already prepared for the training. This time he takes us to a pinnacle. There is a hut he claims to be his home. Outside are training equipments for ladies but none for men.

'Today, before we start, let's meditate for an hour,' he initiates.

An hour is quite dull for me but anyway, Sarah loves to try and me, having no choice but to do. He meditates too this time sitting and facilitates his own way he called 'Anapanasati'. He focuses entirely on his breathe and mind and at times, he will open his eyes to check his posture. He did it in full lotus position and his body is stiff just like a Buddha statue.

As he meditates about 15 minutes, I could see radiance in his face. His skin sparkles and his concentration is so deep that he has into absorption of 'Jhana'. He would not move even if he's shook and he couldn't feel pain even if I would nail him with hundred pounds of hammer.

Anyway I just ignore him and meditate for me, my own training is more important. Sarah is also into deep concentration but at times she would be disturbed by the army of mosquitoes. I can't concentrate well because my mind would linger everywhere and when a mosquito bites, I would feel like smacking it.

The whole one hour meditation ends when master brings himself back from 'Jhanic' state to grounding level. He explains that he had penetrated second stage of 'Jhana'. I was quite wondering what is exactly 'Jhana' but he refused to explain. He wants me to discover myself.

He goes to the training ground where at the back of his house is a pheasant farm. He ties me up both legs and asks me to catch a pheasant. He will take the time. I however feel awkward and start questioning, 'How could I catch a pheasant without limbs?'

Instead, he smiles and asks back, 'How could a snake catch a chicken? Access to your mind and find the answer.'

I start catching the pheasants which are running around. All I could do is to catch feathers. I can only jump around but of course to jump is to distract the pheasants. They will run fly everywhere and it makes things harder. I have to use my mind and unwrapped hands to catch.

Sarah starts her training by finding a pea in a hill of red beans. Master first demonstrate of how fast he could do. He asks Sarah to throw a pea and scatter it around. Master then observes properly how it is scattered. As soon as Sarah finishes, easily he plunges his hand into the red beans pile and picks up the hidden pea.

Sarah was amazed with that trick but she couldn't figure out. Master reminds her not to worry but rather be observant and calm. Being mindful will help those who're nervous.

So master asks her to be ready, he tosses the pea in the red beans pile and, using his leg he messes all over. Sarah has to find patiently.

Meanwhile, I'm struggling to catch a pheasant. I'm panting and sweating but master just looks on, enjoying his tea. Both of us struggling to accomplish our missions. After a few rounds without anything, I decide to untie my legs but the master is too sensitive. He aware of me and quickly toss a small stone at my hand. It hurts and so the master reminds that it will hurt if I try to cheat. He also reminds that no training is easy and we must do it patiently. Sarah on the other hand is so patient finding her hidden pea.

I sit on a bench for a while thinking the master's wisdom, 'How could a snake catch a chicken?' Then, I crack my brain–a snake will glide quietly, using camouflage and agility.

Of course! I could slither among the pheasants and catch them. Besides they are in the farm and not running in the wild! Then, I start to collect the hay in the farm and cover myself. Master then stands up and smiles. He nods which means he knows that I'm starting to use my mind.

I slowly crawl with hay still covering me, none of the pheasant will realize now that I'm approaching. As I'm nearing one of them, I quickly snap its leg and yell 'Eureka!'

The pheasant is in my hand and Master Luo applauses me for my intelligence. Then he approaches me and says, 'Sometimes to fight isn't determined by strength but also by mind. You use the camouflage method and passed but this training I would say stealth method. Well done!'

I bow and thank him and release the pheasant back to the farm. So, I watch Sarah while resting. She is quite tired because of the heat under the sun but anyhow, it is part of the training. Master then whisper to me, 'She must be sensitive enough to find the contrast of color. If she isn't, then she is not good in reaction.'

'But a pea in a pile of red beans, it's tough to find.'

'No, Alex. If you know it is there, then it will be there. But if you scatter all over, isn't it difficult to find?'

'Ah! You're right master.'

Sarah slowly disperses the beans and soon they become leveled. Sarah then detected the hidden pea. Master congratulates her but thinks she needs more training. Later, a monk wearing Tibetan robe appears.

Master Luo greets him, 'Kwa ye Tenzin.'

'Ah kwa ye, Mr Luo. And who are they?'

'My students. They want to learn Kung Fu.'

'Ah, a good practice. Remember when we were . . . ha-ha.'

'Aha-ha. Yes yes sure. The boy is Alex and the lassie is Sarah. Both are couple.'

Master turns to us, 'Alex, Sarah. Why not greet to Venerable, Tenzin Tsungpo?'

So, we greet, 'Good morning Tenzin Tsungpo.'

'Aha . . . good, good. Nice to see you.'

Master interrupts, 'So Tenzin, do you still practice martial arts like before?'

'I do, Luo. But not so much like before. I come here to bring these scriptures from Ñanaka Bodhi Thera. He found this original in a library in Sarnath.'

'Oh that Bhante. He is still strong even in his 80s. I'm amazed.'

'Indeed, but I heard he's currently in New Zealand. Some kind of invitation for Dharma talks.'

'Good to hear that. I can't wait to listen to him. His speech is so powerful that almost everyone will be inspired but just . . . '

'His Sri Lankan accent? Everyone knows that. Ha-ha!'

'Come in Tenzin for rice tea.'

Master prepares the rice tea for three of us and we have a long talk. Tenzin gives some wisdom about life and Master Luo gives his about martial arts. According to Tenzin, he was born in Tibet but has traveled to Japan to learn martial arts. There was once he buries his hatred on the Chinese that he joined the 1959 Tibetan Revolt and filled with bloodlust, he killed two Chinese Red Armies.

Dalai Lama ordered him back, confesses his mistakes and punished him by deserting him so he would think over his mistakes. He took four months to extinguish the defilement in him and asked for forgiveness from the Buddha for he would never be vengeful again. Tenzin also narrated that he used to learn the Theravadan culture of Buddhism that he is excelled in speaking Hindi, Tamil, Sri Lanka and Pāli. That was how he gets along so well with other monks.

His story is quite exciting of how one could face barriers and destroy the mindset of difficulties. He teaches some of his martial arts move that awe us that even Master Luo haven't master. First, he showed the 'Over the Gate Palm' on which he could break a glass behind a watermelon by touching the melon but without hurting. According to him, this move is the psychic phenomenon of the absorption of third 'Jhana' followed by collection of Qi energy. Next he shows the 'Diamond Hand of Avalokishtera (Guan Yin)' that could heal, create intense disappointment or even paralyze a person without contact. Just he shows his palm and murmurs some mantra and the thing would become according to his wish.

He demonstrated on an injured frog which cannot leap. After the stance, the frog leaped as high as it could. He also told us that this move requires the concentration on 'kasina (elemental)' of the nature and also the realization of the highest 'Jhana' because it will cause death if used wrongly.

Lastly before he left us he demonstrated the last technique, 'MahaMoggallana's Shrinking Stance' and like the name of the move, he could size himself into any shape and he also narrated that MahaMoggallana, the second chief disciple of Buddha used this move to defeat the arrogant Naga, Nandopananda. This move requires the full enlightenment of a person. Id est. a person could do that is actually an Arhat.

After me and Sarah were dismissed, we have our lunch at the bar. I chat with Sarah, 'Just can't believe what we saw was like paranormal.'

'Yeah, it's like there is a lot of job to do to equalize his skill.'

We had an enjoyable moment of seeing the skill of someone noble and thoughts come to me–To see is to believe or not, we will never know that our body can do more than anything we thought usual. We are always blinded because of defilement just like dirt covered glass, we will never see through because of the stain. As long as we keep wiping the glass, it will stay crystal clear and we will definitely see through. Just like our mind, we need meditation to the state of purification only then we can observe well our body and go beyond the extraordinary. That is the message Tenzin Tsungpo trying to give to us. A very good teaching indeed and we have to appreciate of everything he meant.

# EPISODE 9:
## TO TRAIN, ENDURE PAIN

Next day of out training is a bit tougher. Master Luo said to achieve something, one should work hard for that because things don't come easy. For him, to have high return, there will be high risk. For once, I thought he uses the economic context to explain things not only the spiritual side. He would command me to find some logs in the forest. He had already scattered the logs which he hacked the whole night to facilitate this training. Sarah on the other hand will rake the hay in the barn using hands only. She must pile them in bushels of ten and for each bushel, the heap would be as high as a tepee.

I found around 5 logs but master told me there will be 7 logs. I must find them, and then pull them to the river. It would be horrendous task to do that alone but master assured me that if I am wise, that will be an easy task. For Sarah, hers will be tough too but Master is training her mindfulness and patience right now just as the first training she did.

When I found the sixth log, I sit there thinking of how to drag them to the river. Then, I thought of helping Rowan out last time but this time, I didn't have a car so I must use some wheels. Indeed the Ancient Egyptians used to find lumbers as wheels and why not I do that my way. I find some smaller lumbers that scattered throughout the forest. About seven in a load will do to cart away these logs. Master is also wise because those scattered logs are actually near to the river–He wouldn't want to make life difficult. So all I need to do is to collect the logs near to the river and later, push them down the river and I will pull to master's training course.

It is not as simple as one thinks it is because the heavy logs actually need to be pivoted to allow the smaller lumber be inserted at the bottom. Then, I need to direct the logs to the river. I must always remember to replace the lumber every time I drag. It takes me sometime to finally push every log to the river. Now I have to jump into the river to direct them to master's training ground. This part is easier because the river is actually flowing to master's place and secondly, these logs are floating, needing lesser work to pull them. The only burden is the current of the river–makes things slow.

Meanwhile Sarah has piled up three bushels. Her hands are made for that because she was born in countryside Tennessee. Master Luo is quite impressed with her speed. He also spotted me dragging the logs with the help of river and he smiles and nods. He is quite happy with our achievement for this time even though the training is tough. He is content with my method of using wheels to support the dragging of those logs.

As Sarah finishes piling up the bushels, she is now needed to burn them down. She has to search for fire woods in the forest and Master Luo already prepared those for her. She also needs to set up by using fire stone. She has to finish collecting the woods before I complete my training. And my training is rather bizarre, cross the floating logs that are already queued up by me and collect the fire stones for Sarah. Mine is rather tougher because I need to personally collect four fire stones with a bag as assistant. Master Luo told us that this isn't using mind anymore but rather agility and aggressiveness, a personality for successful fighter.

Without wasting time, I haste up to search for the stones. Sarah too needs to be quick to collect the woods. Master Luo just muttered, 'They are as good as treasure hunters. Without complain. Impressive.'

I have to cross the logs perfectly. If I fell, I will need to begin from zero that means I need to climb back and run across again. Master will not allow me to cheat and I know he is a good spotter.

Sarah's task will be easier. Collecting those woods and come back waiting for my fire stones. In my mind, Master Luo is quite brilliant as I can see he is actually helping us in the training and every set up is for our importance. In Sarah's mind, she feels like an enjoyable practice as if she was born doing this job. Searching woods is not a difficult task either. The first training already taught her well and Master Luo is so emphasized with this training for her. He wants her to be conscious and next, being responsive wouldn't bring her harm.

Because I kept falling down and couldn't even collect a rock, I'm a bit depressed. Master understands me and approaches me.

'Have you seen the water strider?'

'Yes, master why?'

'They use neither their weigh nor their mind to float on water. They rather use balance.'

'Master? I don't really understand.'

Then, Master Luo demonstrates on the logs.

'I balance up myself in addition of agility and of course with those; I would be able to cross the logs.'

'But master, weight will affect more right like crossing the next one.'

'No. Look properly. I would rather not to use weight for next log but to slow down and stabilize and then only agility comes in. With this balance only I ought to lesser the impact and to cross faster without struggling.'

I try again and this time, when I step on the log, again I couldn't balance and I fall. But it would not lose my confidence and I try another time. To prove balance, I place my two feet and quickly balance myself by spinning the wood and quickly get to the end where I can jump on the next and so forth until I finally cross the river.

I quickly find the stones and bringing them back to Sarah. Sarah has already collected all the woods and about to come back. I have to again cross the logs to reach the piled up bushels but again, losing my balance on the log I fell and losing the stones in the river. Because wet stones couldn't set fire, I have to turn back to find again and this time I'm determined not to make mistakes again.

Sarah is already reaching the heap of hay and I'm still crossing the logs. Looks like Sarah is almost success and master is exultant with her performance. With the determination in me, I crossed the logs as quickly as possible and reach the spot as soon as Sarah arrives.

I lend Sarah a hand to set the fire and when Master Luo approaches, he voices out with stressed tone, 'I wouldn't allow you, Alex to help but how could you do that?'

I stand up, facing the ground. I apologize, 'I'm sorry master. I thought I could help out.'

Master then smiles, 'I encourage team work and if you're gonna be successful, that would be an appraisal.'

I'm delighted with his remarks and help setting up the fire. Master brings out some food and proposes that the training today is part of enjoyable barbeque treat. He got those meats from alms and he roasts them for us. According to him, training sometimes should be enjoyable to make the students happy.

He also reminds us that tomorrow training will be postponed to following day because he would attend a talk by s monk in Hungary besides healing our aching muscle. He also compliments our achievement for today and marks that we have completed the skill of sensitivity, agility, aggressiveness, balance and camouflage.

He told us that although those skills are achieved, we still have to put the focus on them at times. We need to accomplish another four trainings combination of the above and strength that we are yet to learn and only then, we are qualified to the face-to-face training.

My eyes bulge when he said the word 'qualified'. It means for all that we did is just training to build up our body and mind but not the actual sparring part yet. Master would stress that to go for fighting, one should have sufficient warm up and not just to battle so easily. One should know that in which dangerous position he is situated and in some circumstances, one should realize whether to defend or run but never to provoking. The last one is in which circumstances should mind game comes in like using the surrounding as protection factor or to use the means of skills. The most important is not to underestimate the opponents like Dao De-jing said.

While enjoying the feast, Master Luo excuses himself. He wants to go through the scriptures Tenzin gave yesterday. He needs to understand the sutras behind to enable him to participate during the talk tomorrow. I'm eager to learn what is behind the scriptures and so I follow him in. Sarah who is left alone too wants to learn about the scriptures. His room awes us because it is like a library full with spiritual teachings. His room full with books about the Buddha, his Dharma, the disciples and also the biography of Dalai Lama, the Hsing Yun Master and many more spiritual teachers.

When he opens the scroll, he smiles.

'Ah, an original one Kalama Sutta written by a Pāli student. Very good, very good.'

With full of enthusiasm, I ask, 'What is Kalama Sutta, master?'

'A really exciting Sutta taught by Gotama Buddha to the Kalamas during his trip with Kosalans in the town, Kesaputta.'

'So explain, sir. I am keen to know.'

'The Lord was on tour to Kesaputta with large group of monks and in this occasion that the Kalama people appear before him, narrated to him that there are some sages and priests that boasted their teachings and deprecated the others, and so creates doubt and uncertainty. Thus, Buddha told them it is correct for them to doubt which therefore creates uncertainty. And if uncertainty arose, a person should inquire or at least taking the common sense as guidance. He would say, "The contemplatives would be the teacher" and he explained, "If the qualities that we knew to be unskillful, doing so would bring harm to others should we follow then it would lead to suffering. Those qualities in our sense should be abandoned but if otherwise, it should be followed. We shouldn't go by reports, legends, foretold stories, traditions, scriptures or anyone will are relying or of the noble people, the analogies, gossips and even uncertain tales.'

'A good explanation indeed, Master,' Sarah praises with a jovial look.

Then he continues, 'The qualities that could harm others and create sufferings like killing, stealing, to do sexual misconduct, to lie and defame and to induce the others to do such and these will create suffering, that we should abandon. And if arise the thought of greed, hatred and delusion that create the mentioned qualities is what we should not follow. If the teaching is opposite to aforementioned, this is what we should follow and again take contemplatives as the teacher.'

'So it's said to do follow what is skillful is the right thing and to follow the unskillful is the wrong. What happened to the Kalamas after that?'

'It is always right if we do analysis first to judge the good and the bad. Hence, the Kalamas bow to the Buddha, praising his speech and therefore became the laymen who took refuge on his Teaching, the Dharma.'

'Impressive, as if there is nothing to against his preaching,' I compliment.

'Alex, Sarah. It is late now and I hope to teach a few but since tomorrow I need to depart early, it is wise if you go back earlier. I hope you're having fun tonight and as for following day, I will conduct the training only in the afternoon.'

I turn to Sarah. 'It is very fortunate to meet this Master, the person with philosophy and pure heart. I feel ashamed to fight him last time at the restaurant. I think I should apologize if I have insulted him.'

Sarah smiles and places her palm on my shoulder. 'You're real gentleman none I have ever met in my college. How could you keep such a humble thinking?'

'Believe me Sarah. Last time I was arrogant too. I used to go against my Master in Hong Kong Wushu Training Center. When I was a child, I'm ignorant and I like to challenge the others. My Master stood there fiercely and challenged me that he would defeat me in three moves. Because of my ignorance, I accepted his challenge and attacked him. No matter how fierce my moves are, he would be able to block and evade. Finally when I am about to get tired, he just knock me with two moves. One punch on the chest and another kick at my knee and I fell. That's the time I changed, taking his advices and bow down to him.'

'Teachers are always the one to be respected.'

'But after Master Luo talked about that sutra, I believe those who can be trusted are those who teach for the good.'

'Brilliant thinking, brilliant. I agree.'

I walk Sarah to the car and drive home. However, on the way Rowan appears. I have to perform emergency brake. Rowan is roaring fiercely. I have to exit my car when he slams on the hood.

'Wow, wow. What's the matter, Rowan?'

He shows me the head of Kat, Lita and Peter. I'm horrified with that and things are getting serious right now. Rowan transforms himself to a human.

'I saw these in the junkyard.'

'Do you kill Kat and Lita too?'

'Swear not. I saw them there since Peter haven't been back in three days.'

'Where's Felicia anyway?'

'She's hunting me.'

Now the feud is back. Felicia thought that Rowan killed Kat and Lita after finding out Peter has gone. If this is the situation, then it would be difficult to fight the zombies. Rowan nudges me again.

'My highest leader, Hyde will kill her.'

'Who's Hyde?'

'The boss of all Werewolves. They all died out leaving me. I'm the last Werewolf.'

'But you never told me you're the last one. I thought you hunt in pack. You . . . '

'Yes we did. But the battle between us and the Vampires inflicts lots of casualties inclusive the men out there. We need recruit so we won't hesitate to hurt the innocence.'

I don't know the numbers of Vampires out there but I wish to find out how'd that happened. I believe the zombies would be the culprit. I need to go back home too since it's already late at night and I'm already exhausted from the training. I promise him that we'll meet at the same place. He leaps away. The car is now my most feared item because I need to pay the rent and also the car has many scratches and bumps.

I should send to the repairman before paying the rent tomorrow so the owner wouldn't found out the defects behind this 'gorgeous' Prius.

At the hotel's compound, Felicia was there waiting. Two soldiers were slain at both her side. Again I have to get out of my car to deal with her.

Felicia begins, 'I'm sure Rowan had told you what was happening. Are you or are you not believe in him?'

'I can't tell until I find out the truth.'

'Seeker like you takes too much time. Wouldn't it be easy if I kill him straight away?'

'What's the ego in you until things that can be solved, you do it otherwise?'

'An eye for an eye. I believe that is what written in your bible. But that is what carved in my heart, the last descendant of the Vampires!'

'You are the last of Vampires? Rowan too is the last of the Werewolves. Wow, I must be encountering extinction.'

'My queen, the sire Succubus would not let go just like that. She will kill anyone who try to harbor or even protect the enemy.'

'I will see your queen, Felicia. I will solve this between you, Rowan and your bosses.'

Felicia nods and smiles.

'Everything's relying on you, Lex. See you tomorrow, handsome.'

Sarah just laughs. We head back to our hotel and have a relaxing sleep. I wouldn't think much about the business tomorrow. Sarah who is sleeping beside me has fall into her dreamland. She has been so exhausted the whole day and even during the evening.

Next day, new story. New business to do and as always–to resolve conflicts. I don't know what the hell I have done in the past life that I have to be a middle person for every argument. Seems like when thing is about to stop, a new agenda will always come interfering and make things worse. Sarah might ensure me that I have done the right thing. Sarah is always that to comfort. I wish I have the wisdom to accomplish things as fast like my master but I'm still a weaker being.

Like promised, I've gone to meet with the rivals. Sarah is not following because I don't want to lead her to danger situation. Besides, she needs to have a break, researching for the Alamo by going through her previous text books and to practice meditation.

Rowan is already waiting as soon as I arrived at the woods. Felicia is not there maybe due to the sunlight, she is not coming out.

'Look Rowan. I might not have much time but I will try to resolve your conflicts.'

'I know you're the man. Mr. Hyde is in his cavern.'

Rowan leads me to the cavern beyond the woods. It turns out to be an old cathedral, already destroyed by erosion and old age. The door frame has already decayed and at the compound is full with bones, corpse and . . . chemicals. Chemicals?

I feel a bit weird about the place but I build up my courage to enter. The inside of the cathedral is quite large and tidy though the outside, it looks different. The nave has been modified, cleaned up and now, a lab. The piano in the chancel is like a rack for many apparatuses mainly the chemicals. The choir is turned into research area with microscope, Bunsen burner and many tools to conduct experimentation and invention.

Suddenly, someone comes in. Before I can see his real person, he greets. The voice comes from the vestry which has the underground chamber.

'Excellent Alex, excellent. The one who makes his vow finally is not a shadow anymore.'

'You must be Mr. Hyde like Rowan said.'

Then, Hyde appears and he's a normal man. Rowan kneels before him. What made this normal man so feared by the wolves? Why this normal being been hailed as a leader?

'Alex. You saved our clan is it because of the vow that they made or did you do it for fame?'

'I wouldn't trouble myself if nobody troubling me.'

'Straight answer. I like that. I'm wondering too, are you the queer guy I'm looking for?'

'What is that that you want my favor?'

'If you appear to be in the brotherhood, then I need you to bring me the head of that Succubus.'

'So you want the Vampires to disappear after all?'

'Of course, my dear. To show the glory of the wolves, this is your mission.'

'I have a great job and I don't take mission especially if someone wants me to kill. I wouldn't just do that.'

'Rowan might just do that.'

Rowan roars furiously and turns to me. I stare at him with sternly like a warning to make him recall of his vow. But due to Mr. Hyde's command, Rowan just forgets everything. He leaps to me ready to clobber. I did not fight back but rather shoving him away.

Hyde screams, 'Argh! This is no fun! Why don't you fight back?'

I reply, 'Because I am not as evil as you!'

'Just finish him, Rowan!'

I remember master's words to defend myself if I'm in trouble. So I sit down on a stool at the aisle waiting for Rowan to pounce on me. Rowan is charging towards me and I kick on his chest. He falls to the ground but never feel pain. Again he charges and when he strikes, I block and elbow his chest again. I'm trying my best to avoid his nails. He claws again and again and every time he does, I would beat him on his chest.

Hyde becomes terrified with this scenario and he go down the chamber. I am fighting and blocking Rowan's every attack but Rowan seems painless and energetic. Later, Felicia arrives at the cathedral's door. At her side is the Succubus, a beautiful brunette wearing seductive bodice and g-string and a very long black stocking. Her wingspan is as large as an angel but bat-like wings. She is completely whitish but still she is a beautiful person. Everyone caught looking in her red eyes would become 'love bonkers' except for Rowan. I have to really press myself from falling to her.

Felicia quickly teleports to Rowan and shoves him from me. Every time he returns to me, Felicia would beat him up and pushes him away.

I have to voice out to stop the battle.

'Listen both of you!'

Rowan might not listen to me as he's in the rampage form and would approach to claw me but Felicia is blocking him. Suddenly, Hyde appears from the underground chamber, also in the rampage mood and he is Mr. Hyde, a normal human that changes into a Brute after drinking potion! No wonder the wolves are scared of him.

'I will deal with him,' the Succubus offers.

She turns herself into a misty wisp and flows to Mr. Hyde. Then, she starts to beat him on his body in the misty form like a human having stung by bees. Mr. Hyde grows very angry and focuses on the cloud very properly. Then he grabs the Bunsen burner and light up. The Succubus accidentally touches the fire and thrown to the ground. She is scared of fire and so Mr. Hyde pounces on her and bangs her to every edge.

I saw this furiously and grab the stool and strikes Mr. Hyde with might. He felt nothing instead, looks at me and strike me. I am hurled to the ceiling and fall to the ground. The pain is unbearable but due to my training, I must endure it.

The situation turned chaos. Both sides are not listening now. I just hope my master had taught me how to numb their nerves. Suddenly, I have an idea on how to stop them when I noticed the chemicals. I am not a failure in chemistry indeed so I grab some nitric and sulfuric acid and toss to the ground where Mr. Hyde stands.

Feeling the corrosive effect on his foot, Mr. Hyde falls with unbearable pain and slowly changes into human form, turns to me and yells, 'You fucking idiot! You shouldn't do this to your brother!'

I answer cynically, 'I might just do that . . . to him.'

I throw another one to Rowan and he also fell due to extreme pain.

'Now both of you couldn't be in rampage mood because it is painful huh? For your information, my brother wouldn't let me in danger!'

The Succubus flies to Mr. Hyde and claws his neck. Mr. Hyde slowly dies due to excessive bleeding. Felicia turns to me and asks, 'What about Rowan?'

'He is important to me. He will be listening now because of the death of his boss. He should be forgetting the cenotaph right now.'

The Succubus thanks me for my intelligence and together with Felicia and Rowan, they teleport back to their home. Meanwhile as I drive back, I just keep thinking "It is afternoon right now but how could these two came to save me and how could these two knew I'm in danger?"

# EPISODE 10:
## THE PROLONGED ENDURANCE

As soon as I am back, Sarah who is watching TV is so worried. She quickly hugs me and asks, 'How's it going, honey?'

'Very bad indeed. Mr. Hyde is actually Dr. Jekyll. I don't know what is their relationship. I really don't.'

'Ah? I don't understand.'

'There is the Succubus too who is the leader for the Vampires. Everything turns out like a movie screen.'

'Are you going to find out?'

'Sarah, you know my nature.'

'But are you going to make it before we go to America?'

'If you're going to lend your hand and idea, of course I will.'

'You're still able to joke while I am here worrying.'

I am so determined to find out who is the Succubus, the Hyde and also their linkage with the children–Vampires and Werewolves. Perhaps the tomb that I found contains the answer.

I ask Sarah if I would go back to the woods to find the answer and Sarah allows. Obviously I am a busy man finding out the truth and helping the 'needy'. I just hope my hard work pays.

Nearing to the woods, I saw a small man dragging something like a body into the forest. He does it fast and so being curious, I follow him. The dragging trail is actually blood and so smelly it could make me vomit. The person sure to be a killer, and so I speed up to see what will happen to the corpse. He pulls the dead body into the burrow. The burrow is so narrow that only him could be fitted in.

When he is not in the sight, I quickly push myself into the burrow and the burrow is a shallow one. I need to crouch in it. The sunlight could penetrate so I am able to see while crawling. Until one distance, the burrow becomes bigger. The ceiling is high just like a cave and in the inside, the hanging torches helps in traveling inside. The smell of the area just like a déjà vu. I seem to recall the area and smells like I was in the tomb. The drawing on the wall reminds me of the drawing of the wolves but this time, it is drawing of ancient African.

Suddenly, somebody speaks.

'You like the drawing Mister?'

When I look up, it is the 'Loki' guy standing on the podium that fixed to the wall. Then he continues, 'Well, I have wolves and I have ghouls. I tamed both because I hate men. I am Loki the mischief god but I am no evil.'

'What are you talking about?'

'You like the drawing Mister?'

'Why should I like something I don't understand?'

'You see. Egyptians are the trouble and so are people in Africa too. They are black skinned and are in the lowest class in our society . . . '

'Why are you so racist?'

'Hear me bastard! These people deserve to die. They are not of the human class, they are devil!'

'Wow! You're kinda Ku Klux Klan huh?'

'I have learned the voodoo from the Bantus and now I killed them. They are alive as the zombies and they served me. Ha-ha-ha!'

'What the hell?'

'The Fenrirs will fight along with me and I killed Kat and Lita to bring the attention of the Vampires so the Wolves would be eliminated as they are not sincere!'

I'm queered by his statement. His mission is to destroy the Hyde so the Wolves will not have a leader. If their leader gone, the Wolves would not be able to hunt in pack and so they did rampage to the people.

'So did you kill Peter, Nick and Nikolay too?' I ask.

'Oh I am. I throw the meat for the zombies to bait you but you're lucky that you escaped.'

'So you did everything in the junkyard so we could be trapped by the zombies?'

'Not really but the Ghoul Lord! Ha-ha-ha!'

Now I think I am in trouble. The cave may be the hive for the zombies and as I am here, I wouldn't be able to escape. Loki chants something and when he shows his ring, the strong wind blows away the torches except the one on the podium. Soon, the living dead spawn from the ground and there is one big one almost like I saw, the giant zombie. This one is shitless and super muscular. His head is like a rock but smaller but his arms size is like a tree trunk. Loki addresses him the 'Ape Zombie'. His mouth is so smelly like the smell of million corpses. When he takes a step, the ground shakes violently.

Loki later commands, 'The Goliath had died because of him and his company. This man owes us a life and now, payback time by enjoying his flesh.' Loki later disappeared.

I quickly turn back and faster crawl to the narrow tunnel. The other zombies are chasing too but I manage to exit despite the dark tunnel. I quickly jump out to the open space and the other zombies are also struggle to come out. I grab a wood and hit them very hard on their head if they manage to appear from the burrow.

One by one the zombie's heads are smash by me until I hear the hard stomping sound. Some zombies are thrown to the burrow's entrance and it must be the Ape Zombie that is coming near. I quickly find a pointed stake so I could impale his head before he comes out.

There are a lot of pointed sticks but none are strong enough. The Ape Zombie breaks open the ground and toss a big rock towards me. I duck and roll to a tree for cover and the rock missed me. The zombie could pull out the trees to go after me and so I need to be quick planning of how to knock him down before he terrorized the whole forest. Of course there is something useful in the trunk.

I run through him while he is pulling a tree and quickly head to my car. It is chasing me violently throwing anything on me and so I have run in zigzag to evade. If I device my plan, I would need a chain and lubrication oil which are all inside the trunk.

Because the zombie is fast and there are many more which are coming out from the burrow so I quickly grab the chain, the padlocks and the oil. The zombie throws another rock but luckily it doesn't hit the car. I run from that area and faster run to an area where two trees are near to each other. I chain both trees and pour some oil over that area. Then I run through a narrow gap produced by fallen trees and this could at least hold the zombie for a while as he needs to break through the trees to chase me. I have to find some fire stone in the area and it is the best to find it around the burrow. All I have to do is to take a round to go back to the burrow.

I need to be quick in my actions before the oil dries out. So I run back while the zombie is cracking the trees and I haste up to get out of his sight. The zombies are wandering at the burrow and I need to melee with them. I grab one sharp stick and charge at them. One by one are impaled on the stake until I take some fire stones from the burrow. The Ape Zombie is still tracking me while I dip some oil on the stick. I quickly light a fire by using the fire stones and it is a tough job. I need to be fast whereas torching with fire stones needs time.

I put in more strength until I see some spark. Hence, I light up nearer and as the spark touch the oil, the fire lights up. I am so relieved because I manage to light up before the Ape Zombie finds me. He is nearer and he senses me when I began to wave the fire. I quickly distract him to make him follow me. I run towards the oil patch where I chained the trees. Some zombies that are not killed follow me too. They chase me towards the oil patch too.

When I see the chain, I jump over and avoid the oil patch but the Ape Zombie tripped and fall. With the burning stake, I impale on his head and the fire spread when contact with the oil patch. The other zombies too fell into the fire and all of them are burnt to ground. The Ape Zombie is still alive but is weakened and the flame eventually kills him.

I return to my car, drive back to downtown and have it fixed at a repair depot. The repairman is fast enough to repair my car so I could drive to the garage and pay my rental.

'Man, I thought you would never come. I could've called the policia you know?' the car owner grumbles.

'I'm sorry. Here's 620 leu for this week right? Next week will be the last.'

'That I will take care with the deposit. Have a nice day.'

Sarah who is waiting for me cheer up when I come back, still breathing. She is eager to know what makes my jacket so dirty. And now I narrate about the stunt behind defeating the zombies and when I mentioned about Loki, she is surprised that every trick is done by him. She shakes her head as Loki is really the trickster god.

We really have a new assignment–to nab the Loki before serious tragedy going to occur. Rowan who is under the Vampires custody must understand the situation now. Everything bad is because of Loki's plan and he did for Ghoul Lord. I can't understand why he works for the Ghoul Lord.

Sarah told me she has contacted Percy Goddard, a lecturer who has studied the Alamo. The meeting will be held as soon as we reach Texas. I am so happy to hear that because she could find someone to interview in a short time. I am so joyful with the strength she has to help me in completing the column. Later, Mr. Barry calls.

'Hello Alex and Sarah.'

'Hi boss,' Sarah replies.

'I'm so glad that your column about the Medieval has made the best. Keep up the good work on the Alamo too. I wish to say well done for your work.'

'Thank you sir. I will be in Texas next week,' I answer.

'Yes sure. I will book a hotel for you.'

'Make sure only one hotel room,' Sarah says.

'Huh . . . 'Mr. Barry is a bit confused.

'Thank you. Bye bye,' Sarah quickly hangs up.

I look at Sarah disbelieve.

'What was that you told him?'

'A plan for closer relationship,' Sarah smiles.

Should she consider me her boyfriend or what? I'm lazy to think and I dare not ask too. I am quite tired actually due to the game with the zombies. After shower, I take a nap by the balcony. The time is 3 p.m. and Sarah has gone for shopping.

Only 15 minutes my nap was, my phone rings. I pick up my cell phone and hear the familiar voice. The voice that used to threaten me and the voice from déjà vu. Again it irritates me but this time it doesn't sound hostile. It sounds like someone needing a help.

'Shut up, don't answer me,' he begins. 'Your car is at the bottom. Your girlfriend has been kidnapped.'

'Hello?'

'I said shut up! Now grab the wheels and drive to the burrow!'

I quickly go downstairs, exit the lobby and drive my car which is parked at the porch and drive to the woods. I park nearby the burrow and the person appears from behind a tree. He wears a cloak, a rag and his face is fully covered like a ninja. He also wears a sash with many potions hanging and he is tall and thin like a gnarled tree.

'Well, you've come back. I am the Oracle. Usually when I do things, I accept payment but this time I did it for free. Since you and Master Luo are students and teacher, I am appreciating this relationship.'

'Where's Sarah?'

'Loki has taken her deep into the burrow. He's quite displeased you've killed the zombies and the two special ones. He has captured her but I don't know for what purpose. Be careful of the third one zombie in this burrow.'

'The third one?'

'I am the Oracle, the Master of the Nature and I can sense everything especially one who closed to Master Luo. I am his actual guardian. Of course I know where Sarah was. She is deep inside the burrow almost the catacombs.'

'Thank you. I will hurry.'

'No! The third special zombie named the Glutton is an extreme eater. It acts like a bulldozer to things getting in its way. Remember; defeat him by his name not by martial arts.'

'Okay. I will remember.'

'Yet I need to pass you these,' he passes me two canisters of powder and an envelope.

'What are these?'

'Only open up when you're in the critical situation.'

The Oracle didn't answer me but disappears when he travels deep into the woods. I quickly get into the burrow and crawl through the tunnel. It seems like the torches are dazzling again. I climb on the podium where the Loki guy was hiding after summoning the zombies. The place is dark when seen from outside the podium so I get a torch from the hanging place. I follow the hollow which is a long winding cave until the dead end. I thought I have got into the wrong turning but as I know the hollow is just a one way. Suddenly, I hear footsteps on the ceiling. It appears like thud on the plank. Perhaps, I am below a secret passage. As I go nearer the sound, I could feel dirt falling to the ground and slowly I push open the plank. It produces soft creaking sound. As I tilt the plank to some degree, I could peep through and I can see it is a mass ritual where any people are gathering there wearing wolf's skin.

Later, the Loki arrives with Sarah being bound to a stake. She is made to stand at a pillar and Loki commands the horde to silent.

'Today is the day the destiny awaited. The day I'm so proud of and the day I'm announcing the wedding ceremony.'

Oh wow! He grabs Sarah which is considered kidnapping pulls her into the cave, an ugly scenery, having her tied and announced this is a wedding? He should be great . . . and weird.

Sarah screams, 'This is not a wedding. It's a threat and I'm not going to marry you!'

'Yes you are. What did I miss? I have spectators, I have witness and they are them.'

'You have nothing, idiot! You don't have a priest, bouquet and my relatives! This is totally unacceptable!'

'Quite right you are. I am the priest. They are your relatives and we need to . . . snatch some flowers and suitable gown for you.' Then he turns to the crowd and announces, 'Look! I need some men to grab some flowers and proper wedding gown for her! Do it now and the ceremony will be on tonight! For now, I'm sorry to announce that this ceremony is cancelled for now! Dismiss!'

The crowd starts to disperse and I wait until the area is clear only I push myself out. The crowd is heading towards the passage where Loki and Sarah were first to move through. I sneak behind the crowd and they are actually heading to the catacombs. Further from the catacombs is a dungeon with cells on the four side of the corner. Two 'wolf' guards are guarding the area. They are holding shotguns. Sarah is forced to go inside the cell by one of the guards but when noticed by Loki of his roughness, he slaps that guy. He utters, 'Be a gentleman to my wife-to-be'

Then he walks into a chamber at the edge of the catacombs. The sculpture is Gothic with the doors of primeval state Venetian style. When the other underlings are out of sight, I am to attract one of the guards. I toss my burning torch to the ground and one of them realizes. The guard moves from his position and investigates the sound and found out it's just a burning torch. From his back, I attack him silently by choking him and knock his head very hard to the wall. He fainted there and we switch our clothing.

I quickly grab his shotgun and drag him back to the guard.

'Look, I've a trespasser. Quick, open up the cell and throw him in!'

Being obsequious, he opens up the cell and I throw him in. He looks up at me and praises, 'Well done my friend.'

I just answer, 'By the way, he is your friend too.'

'What . . . '

I box him twice on his face until he faints too and both of them are locked up in the cell. I grab his keys and open Sarah's cell. Obstinate Sarah refuses to come out.

'Beast of Loki, I wouldn't be persuade by you!'

Realizing I'm wearing the wolf's skin and mask, I remove it and Sarah became rejoiced with my appearance. I give her the stripped guard's clothing so she could disguise as one of them too and we sneak through the obstreperous dining room where the underlings are enjoying feasting. Loki was seen uttering the words like 'Heimdall', 'Valkyrie' and 'Einhenjar'.

I wish I know who are they and when we pass through, we reach the Crypt which is the end of the catacombs. The Crypt is on a higher ground from the catacombs which need us to climb about 145 steps of narrow staircase. I thought it will be good if I escape through the burrow but I am already late. Some of the men are heard exiting the dining room and we have to go to the Crypt. Spider web are everywhere and the place is not maintained. The Crypt is like the place for the royal because treasures are seen everywhere. The place contains tiaras, gold, diamonds and crowns and maces or maybe stolen items.

Because the place could produce echo, I warn Sarah not to obtrude herself so we walk very slowly. Every step must be done very slowly and carefully to obviate any danger of being noticed or tumbling down. When finally we reach the Crypt, things turned unpleasant. From the inside is the dwelling of zombies. Some of them wandering aimlessly and some of them are gnawing the bones. If we are clumsy, we will be end up as their dinner or if a bit of luck, we are only the captive in the cell.

The Crypt is odorous but we have to strengthen ourselves to be a survivor. It is dark and really unpleasant place. We must be careful not to attract a single zombie or it would be an off-day for us. Me and Sarah have the modern shotguns with seven canisters in each so we only have 14 rounds to depend on.

Luckily I remember the envelope before we move on. In the envelope contains a letter saying, "To thee who art the bravest, thou art assigned to destroy the enemy of the Kings, the Glutton. Light the powder that easily ignites when touches the heat and should thou implode the Glutton. Upon his death shall the Kings obsequies be in peace."

Maybe the powder is squib graphite. I pour them all the way passes the zombies stealthily and until a distance, I could hear a soft growling sound from opposite a hollow. At my back there is another diverged hollow and I can see sunbeam from here. The ground quakes with stomping sound and with another canister left I quickly creep forward the radiant area. It is a shallow hole and I ask Sarah to quickly climb up.

The Glutton has sensed me and charging forward. I shoot at the powder and explodes violently produces loud bang. The fire becomes wilder and is razing the Crypt as some zombies are burned to death. The Glutton still survives and is coming after me. It gnashes at us and when anything that obstruct its way will be stroke off and anything that it got a hold on would be devoured even though it's a zombie. It functions almost like a whale, a rampage zombie. It is far hungrier than the first and second special zombie.

Enough of the objects swallowed, it will burp out disgusting smell and vomit some hazardous sticky substance. When contact with the wall, it will eventually crack. This zombie eats non stop and is considered very dangerous. So I have to throw the squib canister to him and if blessed, I should have blown the canister with my shotgun.

I bet on my life with this only chance and if I failed, the whole world is gone. So I toss the canister into its mouth and fire two shots but missed. I'm in total disaster right now as it has eaten the canister! I quickly run out, not to look back again. The zombie is chasing after us and also the rest of the smaller ones. However, suddenly it stops. It feels a little irritate like bees stinging him. Later, the belly explodes and flesh scatter everywhere. The substance burst out and sticks together all the smaller zombies eventually melting them. The squib powder actually works with the substance during digestion and is reactive when the zombie starts chasing us!

Now I have accomplished this mission and run out of the underground Crypt and get out to the woods but luck only sits with me temporarily. The wolf guards caught us at the entrance and take us back to the cell.

# EPISODE 11:
## RESCUE? 'ON THE WAY, IN MY MIND'

We were thrown into the cell and Loki is laughing cynically.

'It is still early for you Sarah. Someone is getting a nice gown and you will be my wife for tonight.'

I just grin at him. I know someone will come for rescue and after that, he will be end up in prison too. I just test him by asking, 'What do you want from us?'

'All ever I wanted is to revive the Ghoul Lord, live happily ever after with my wife, Sarah and had your head be thrown to Scandinavia.'

'Well . . . good if you can do that. But how are you going to revive the Ghoul Lord if it's already dead.'

'That is rather quite brusque to say the Ghoul Lord is dead. He is not. I just need the heart of Sarah, the pure sweet heart of loving which is good enough to revive the Ghoul Lord. That's it.'

'Wow. Incredible. You marry her to be sacrificed and what will happen if the Ghoul Lord is revived?'

'Then I'm the king of the world, rules over the zombies and to those who are living will eventually infected and of course you too! No survivors and everyone are listening to me! The treasures are mine and Sarah, you too! Ha-ha-ha! Next is the Ghoul Lord will be my advisor and will grant me three wishes! Three deadly wishes! I am the God, Loki and will be the strongest of all!'

'I know now what did you mean by happily ever after. And what will happen to the wolves if you turned them into zombies?'

'That . . . will be considered,' he whispers.

He is quite lucky the wolves never heard him. Then he locks up the cell and marches away with the guards. Two guards come to look after our cell. Sarah of course was shocked by Loki's statement but I assure her to be brave.

Me and Sarah start to plan how to trick those guards again. Sarah is really in danger as the cankerous Loki will have her heart gauged out to be offered to the Ghoul Lord. This time I think of Sarah to attract them with voluptuous style. Me, on the other hand pretend to constipate.

At first the guards are not attracted but after persuasions from Sarah, one of them has a look. I fake myself of being so painful, having serious constipation that the guard now obliged to open up the door. I request him to come nearer because I want to whisper something for him but he ignores. Sarah again makes herself voluptuous and tries to attact him and this time he ogles at Sarah and from the back, I throttle him and Sarah quickly grabs his shotgun and knock him unconscious. The other guard heard the noise and charges in. I quickly hook his leg and Sarah again knocks him with the gun's butt and he too becomes unconscious.

This time I clinch Sarah's hand and with the shotgun on another we head back to the burrow's exit. There are two dwellings chatting at the burrow's edge and I have no choice but to fight them. I bash one of them and kick the other while Sarah hit them with the shotgun. I found out they have daggers are kept in the sash.

I would grab those blades in case of emergency and we head towards the burrow. We run down from the podium, towards the exit. It goes shallower and we need to crouch back up there and with the guidance with only moonlight, we climb back up to the woods. There my loyal car is waiting, untouched but I think someone had triggered the guards and the wolf dwellers are chasing after us.

It is coincidence too that the Succubus is waiting for me leaning at my car and the Oracle is there.

The Oracle speaks, 'Now you've found out what is behind his tricks. You've got to be careful.'

'The troops are coming out now. We've got to bury them!'

The Oracle then throws some serpents inside, 'These will handle them.'

I turn to Succubus and ask, 'Ah, what now?'

'Rowan needs help.'

Without further question we go to the Succubus' place. Hers is at an old church with cemetery at the compound. Beside are Mausoleum and a large obelisk with epitaph written on. The beacon is so unstable and looks like it will fall in a mean time.

The Succubus leads us towards the underground and it is actually a morgue. Felicia is standing opposite Rowan who is restrained to the wall. She has been guarding him the whole night and Rowan has been struggling to free himself. Rowan is so bloodlust when he saw the Succubus and struggles to hurt her. I know Rowan had a very bad day since Mr. Hyde was killed. So I approach him.

'I'm so sorry if I have to do it. I didn't mean to and so is she.'

Rowan stops struggling and starts to listen.

'Look Rowan. I am doing this because we're tricked. Loki, he pranks us into this game. He wants you dead since you already disobey him. He wants us dead!'

The Succubus inquires now, 'And why the Hyde wants you dead too?'

'This is what I need to find out.'

Felicia releases Rowan but he is still hostile with her. I have to relax him so nobody will get hurt. The Oracle suddenly speaks out.

'This place is where a tome was kept. It tells the origination of you, the monstrous trio. I believe Succubus, Hyde and Ghoul Lord are not the leader of the Vampires, Werewolves and zombies respectively but someone else. They are the vassal to the king of the medieval times. I believe each of them has the title Hersir or Jarl.'

'What makes you think this way?' Felicia asks.

'Loki is the god of the Vikings. After the raiding of Vikings to the Roman which soon the whole of the Europe falls into the barbaric era, it has significance with the belief the Loki guy has right now. Anyhow, Alex, you've found out that the Werewolves have relationship with the Egyptians and I believe this legend has bought either way from the Ottoman or the Roman to the Europe. Secondly, I believe the voodoo tradition too was bought from somewhere Africa to the Europe and if not mistaken, through ritual of the City of the Dead, the rising of the ancestral or by the practice by Bantu nomads. And of course, the Vampires are origination from the Europe and assimilation with the Egypt of reviving the dead.'

'Woo! Your explanation seems rather obscure despite at times, I can see the relationship. Now a little bit obfuscate. Whatever, we will have to move on, trick the little trickster into our trap and have you, Mr. Oracle to reward him a little lecturing,' the Succubus suggests.

.'That is a great idea but right now, I'm so tired,' Sarah yawns.

Rowan who is already in the human form groans, 'If there is no association between the death of my boss and Loki, I would clobber off all of you.' Then he exits from the morgue.

I agree with Sarah that we've really used up much energy to escape from Loki and tomorrow will be our training with Master Luo and I hope we are having a good sleep tonight. I am not thinking further of defeating Loki neither do Sarah. Even the Oracle has disappeared and I'm wondering who is the masked mercenary that helped us to destroy the Glutton.

The next day, a really tough season as we are brawling face to face with Master Luo. In the afternoon, we drive to the meet, his very own home and in the barn, he is waiting. His hands are holding two cudgels and his face is very serious this time.

'Bodhidharma taught of Shaolin reminded that his martial art needs the combination of agility, balance, strength, aggressiveness, concentration and quick thinking. Always the nature as your guide but sometimes, your mind too needs to be sensitive. What if you are blind? You need to fight too. I'm now here blinding myself and both of you deal with me.'

He tosses both the cudgels for us and covers his eyes. It is complete handicap for he is blindfold, unarmed, two on one and he's older than us. We quickly surround him and he only listens to the footsteps. Sarah who is at his back does the first move by striking at his waist. He sensed of that and evade by twisting his body a bit to allow the cudgel through so Sarah missed the hit and I'm aiming his head but when I sweep, he could hear me. He just hunches a little and I completely miss the target.

Sarah again charges up to him this time hoping to hit his stomach but he could sense her coming and readily to block her strike by using his hand and with the opportunity he has, he just shoves Sarah by only his palm. Sarah's cudgel has fallen to his hand. I take the opportunity by striking his legs. Due to the noise of sweeping on the ground, he could spot my position and retreats. None of them hit his leg and when I do it more furiously, he just kicked me on the face and his right leg steps on the cudgel so strong that I couldn't move it. We are defeated though it's a handicap match.

Master then takes off his eyes cover and stares at us angrily.

'When I think of something special, I need to wait a hundred years. Both of you dealing with me eyes uncovered, with weapons and the most important, two of you but none can even bring me to the ground. What is happening?'

We just kneel down speechless and it is quite shameful with the scene like that that we couldn't bring down an old man.

Master than sits down on a rock with a bit remorse on his face preaches, 'To fight, you must have team work and the most important is not to underestimate your opponent. Have I not told you that?'

We just nod. And he continues, 'Always see your weakness, discover and change and this is how you fight! You're dealing not with me but rather challenging yourself.'

He stands up and walks to and fro while preaching, 'When you fight with me, you became impatient and that is the first weakness. Sarah, Alex, I don't see the necessities of you charging up to me like a wild boar you know. That is too rushing and of course you will be trapped by that attitude. I of course could hear the sound you made and spot your position and that makes you wondering how could I defeat all of you so easily.'

I timidly ask, 'Master, you mean we should slither?'

'You should evaluate for yourself. If it is good to slither then you should. If both of you were to strike simultaneously, it may be good to slither.'

I am willing to try again this one on one with him. I grab a cudgel and Master, he just raise his both hands. He is not blindfolded now and we start. Both of us are rather static this time each taking the advantage of the surrounding. I move nearer to him but he never fidgets. And I stride closer but still he never moves. Quickly I strike with the cudgel, aiming his abdomen but he could avoid. So the battle is on, I keep on hitting but every time I did, he would avoid and knock me back. I couldn't just give up and keep on striking him. His repulsive movement actually brings me to the stalemate but I just wouldn't give up. His calmness then absorbed into my mindset and now I could actually think of blinding him. There's just the clod behind him. If I could make him retreat perhaps I could defeat him.

Again I do violent striking on him and he evades. After a few steps backward, I kick the clod on him and actually blinding him as the dust and dirt is floating around him. The impact of 'flash bang' gives me the chance to hook his legs and bring him down. Then I point one end of the cudgel at him making him admitting defeat.

He stands up this time with a smile carved on his face, he congratulates. Then he asks, 'What would it be if our mind is clearer now? Will any blockage ever be your barrier?'

I didn't answer but smile. Sarah then stands up and this time I could see her spirit. She challenges Master Luo. She wouldn't use any weapons but rather her own two hands. Master smiles meaning he accepts her challenge.

As Sarah is prepared, she steps closer to master and first she swipes a few punches on him but none landed his body. When the last punch almost touches his chest, he just jumped a few steps backwards. Sarah then calms herself again. Again she moves closer and when ready, she drops a few kicks but also none lands on him.

Sarah controls her aggravated self and now focus on every movement she could possibly defeat him. She notices that if she makes him slip for every step he retreats, she could probably bring him to ground. So the first thing is she tries to punch him on the upper of his chest and his face and he retreats again. When he stops, Sarah now kicks his abdomen but missed. Until he stops again, Sarah takes the opportunity by quickly hook his leg. When he jumps up, Sarah punches on his stomach and the first time her strike is on the target. Master Luo is still standing and smiling.

Sarah notices now that he is standing in from of a fallen tree and any wrong movement could result in someone falling to ground. Sarah seeing this quickly claws him but again he avoids and when he does, Sarah perform a back kick and again Master Luo avoids by bending himself backwards. Sarah lowers herself and double punches his abdomen and successfully hit him. With another kick on the abdomen eventually makes him retreats more and this time already touches the trunk and he's about to fall. Sarah charges up almost clawing his face that he started grip on Sarah's hand. Then he laughs with well done words uttered from his mouth. He's also jubilant that we have graduated.

'How'd you feel after defeating me, Sarah?'

'I'm so proud and satisfied. I feel no longer fear of anything including that Loki guy.'

'Indeed my friend. If your mind is clear, clear of fear and rid of unwholesome thoughts, eventually you will know for yourself who you are. This is the last of the training and good luck in your trip to America.'

I stop him, 'Master! You couldn't just let go us. What about the higher training?'

'Remember what I've preached about the tree and the leaves? That is my job and I've accomplished for all of you has attained the basic?'

'Alright. But master, I want to ask . . . '

'The Oracle? He's my greatest disciple and he comes to help you because you have accessed his Metaphor.'

'He's only Metaphor?'

'Yes. He's non existing kind of mindset only generated by me. I ask him to help you because I've sensed danger even I was in Hungary. Now I know you can protect yourself. You will no longer needing us.'

We bow to him simultaneously but when we look up, he is already disappeared. Sarah looks at me with wonder but I just utter, 'Don't be surprised. He always did that.'

Sarah then responds, 'Guess that's the last we will ever glance of him.'

That night when we are celebrating the 'graduation' by taking a stroll by the hill, Rowan appears. I am queered at his appearance then asked, 'What an unexpected invitation, Rowan? Are you stalking on us?'

Rowan grunts softly, 'Take me to America.'

Sarah is awestruck with that statement. She crosses her arms and asks, 'What major business do you have in America?'

'I believe there are some of my clans there, Heidi is the one.'

Unbelieving, I question this time, 'How? How do you know you have the clan there?'

'I just think. I'm not sure either. I've heard the tales of the Indian and I want to meet them to stop Loki from reviving the Ghoul Lord.'

'I'm going to Texas, not any place of North America, Rowan.'

Suddenly, Felicia and Succubus fly over.

'Too unfortunate, Alex that the Ghoul Lord is resting in peace in Texas too,' Felicia speaks and turns to Rowan, 'I wish to lend a hand, Rowan but if you want us to teleport you over, I think I might not be able.'

Then a bit frustrated and voice out, 'What are you all up to? If we bring you to America, then I am endangering the people there!'

'I promise you this will never happen. After we destroy the Ghoul Lord, we will quickly return. We will never harm anyone there.'

'Promise yea. It's not like I have never tried to convince myself,' I speak of that while glaring at Rowan.

Sarah interferes, 'How should we take you there? We will be boarding soon and we don't have enough money to buy everyone of you a ticket.'

'Don't worry, Sarah,' Felicia convinces. 'We can't appear in the mid of the sun too.'

'So how are you all going to depart to America?'

'We teleport into the plane. Basically you just take Rowan with you.'

I raise my eyebrow then test them, 'You mean we are bootlegging you?'

'I suggest so,' the Succubus answers.

The mixed feeling of dilemma and fear comes to my nerve. I'm quite hesitate to approve because I can't be sure of the purpose behind them but since they are ardor to defeat the Ghoul Lord and they have shown sincerity then I suggest them to teleport Rowan too to the luggage cabin since I couldn't fund him.

Succubus agrees and Felicia too. Rowan is quite hostile but after I persuade then he also agrees. Before we dismiss, I ask, 'What about Loki, Succubus?'

'Have you heard the idiom if there is the will, there is the way? He is on the way to America right now.'

I'm appalled with that.

'How so?'

'With the flight I guessed. I don't know.'

I promise them that I will get the flight tickets as soon as I contact Mr. Barry later and we will depart to Texas. When everything is okay, they dismissed and me and Sarah drive back home.

As soon as I'm at the hotel, I quickly contact Mr. Barry.

'Hello, boss.'

'Hello Alex. Good to hear from you.'

'Mr. Barry, have you booked our hotel. We need them tonight.'

'What time you will be going, son?'

'Evening at 8. Will it be good?'

'Sure. We will do it pronto!'

He hangs up and Sarah who is anxious asks about the conversation. I look at her with smile and she knows the meaning and hugs me.

Suddenly when I think of the wind of change, only in a day mixed feelings come haunting us. Sometimes pleasant and sometimes unpleasant. Like we have finishing the training with Master Luo and thought that this has ended the mission yet new mission has come and the unsettled ones are waiting to be accomplished.

When thought back of his words, it's quite true 'Why one should be so joyful when he is lucky and why should one be so sad if he's jinx? These are ups and downs of life and if our mind is calm, we could see clearly who we are and how we stand. For that phenomenon, it is just like a wind of change, sometimes blowing sometimes calm. For every hill, there will be valley but we are still living.'

# EPISODE 12: THE FINAL TRICK

Still can't believe of what they said about Loki, I drive to the burrow again the very dawn. Sarah is still enjoying her dream. It is only 6 o' clock that I arrive at the burrow. The place is complete mess. The burrow is covered with mud and it seems like has been collapsed just recently. I move a little bit further to the Crypt and also messed up like have been bulldozed all over. The tomb stones are scattered everywhere and the entry to the Crypt is clogged with debris. If I really going to move the debris, it will take the whole day so I'm not going to excavate.

I drive again to the tomb where I first found out about the Werewolves history. The tomb has just disappeared. The hole is perfectly covered and not even a trace of tangible hollow could be detected. With the hopeless decision of making another adventure deep inside the tomb, I head back to my hotel.

At the motel where I was first registering, I find the Gypsy old man to tell him of our last day here. He asks me to refer to Gerard Rosicky. So I call to his extension but he is not in the line. The

Gypsy old man is obliged to take charge then to proceed with my checkout procedures.

Back to my room, Sarah is still sleeping as the time is only 8 a.m. I peck on her cheek and call up the hotel service for breakfast set. Then I walk to the couch and have a nap. About 15 minutes, the hotel service calls up and I answer the door. Two breakfast sets are ready and with as lowest as possible, I prepare them besides the bed and pay the man some tips too. I eat one set and another as a surprise for Sarah.

When she wakes up, I am sitting by her side smiling. She smiles back with a radiant look.

'Good morning honey and I have this surprise for you,' I greet and holding a plate of delicious breakfast plate.

'Wow, nice smell and tasty too.'

'You enjoy that, dear while I'm going to hit the shower.'

While she is having a blissful moment hitting the shower, suddenly someone calls my room. Sarah picks up.

'Hello, Mr. Chrasoom?'

'I'm sorry. Do you mean Mr. Chrimson?'

'Yes I am. I am Mr. Rosicky, the old man who looks after the motel at the back. My son, Gerard is managing the hotel that you stay.'

'Oh hi there. Alex is having a shower and I am his girlfriend, Sarah.'

'Sarah, could you tell Alex to call me. The extension is 12'

'Certainly, Mr. Rosicky.'

Sarah is quite queered about the trembling old man's voice. He seems like frightened by something or worrying. She is quite questioned by his stress.

So when I finished showering, I ask Sarah who has phoned me. Sarah says that it is the Gypsy old man that called me, Mr. Rosicky. He asks me to call back as soon as I've showered to his extension. So I did.

'Hello, Mr. Rosicky.'

'Hello. Is this Mr. Chrimson?'

'Yes I am. What is the matter with the tizzy voice?'

'Gerard is gone.'

'What? Where was the last time you saw? When was the last he is here?'

'Last two days, he told me he will be in the golf course and later with his private plane; he will be going to Bulgaria to visit his aunt. He said he will be back but until now he hasn't called. His aunty said he has already departed and surely he's already home yesterday.'

'Where is his house?'

'Just around the resort after passing the forest.'

'I think I know where it is.'

'You know where is him now?'

'I mean . . . I know his house.'

'Of course I know his house. He's my son. I will take you there.'

After changing my clothes, I rush to the receptionist and there the old Rosicky is waiting. So we rush to Gerard's house. The place is so quiet. The hall is ransacked but nothing seems to be taken. The Plasma TV is still brand new sitting on the desk. The shelves are also ransacked and jewelries are scattered everywhere. Nothing is taken away and there is no motive of robbery. Later, I traced of footprints leading to a room. I quickly go over and when I open the door, Gerard is tied up and gagged on his bed. He's struggling to release himself. His clothing is quite nice and he's not hurt either.

Sarah immediately releases him and when asked, he described that there are several men kidnapped him when he's on the way back to hotel.

'One of them, the leader asked if I have a plane. I tried to deny but his companion threatened to kill us; me and my driver. They are armed with shotguns and they dress like freaky wolves or something,' he said.

'I think it's Loki!' Me and Sarah exclaimed.

'Yeah, yeah. He said too that he's Loki and if I refuse to help, I will be damned. They need the plane so hurry but I didn't know what is the purpose behind. I still decline to speak out until of them found out it is in my private airstrip behind my house. Loki asked a guard to tie me up and they hijacked my plane and flew away. They captured my driver because he knew the driver could fly the plane. The plane is my favorite gift but now, it is gone! I wish I know where they are now.'

'Don't worry. I know where is his location. Your flight will be back soon.'

At night, I return the rented car to the owner and catch a taxi to the Otopeni airport. Rowan, Felicia and the Succubus are waiting there. After checking which exit should I be, we are told that the plane already waiting in Exit 11 which is a Boeing flight.

I remind, 'Look here. We will be departing with that Boeing 747. You try to sneak into the luggage compartment, should be at the bottom and after the landing, stay calm not to be spotted.'

'Aye sir. We actually know what to do. Don't worry.'

'That is what I'm worrying.'

Hence, immediately they teleport to the plane while we proceed to the custom check and ticket verification only then we enter the plane.

The flight takes about 4 hours to reach Dallas. Mr. Barry contacted us that he had booked the Dallas Hotel for us. About those guys, they need to find their shelter. So when we landed, I ask them to search for shelter. Rowan says he has no problem for he will find Heidi. The Succubus and Felicia will be in trouble because there will be no casket for them so they decide to hide in graveyard.

Rowan comes with us to the hotel until midnight. We travel to the forest and he howls. Heidi suddenly appears from no where. She is quite pretty. She is red haired with white strip at the fringe and she wears all white. Her skin is tanned and she looks like mixed Caucasian. She is Native mothered type of shewolf.

She thanked me when we meet and she is quite polite. She also assures that Rowan is safe in the hands of the Indians and she is a vegetarian wolf. Later she transforms into white wolf (not a partly human) and they disappear in the forest.

For the Succubus and Felicia, they found an abandoned burial ground next to a craggy hill. The Succubus is satisfied for the ground is a perfect hideout for them. It is not disturbed and calm for resting in peace during the day. At the middle lies a cenotaph for the soldiers fought for the Texian army.

Meanwhile the Loki is busy locating the Ghoul Lord. They need to find a map which believed is located in somewhere Dallas too. We are too tired to trace them so we have a rest at night in the hotel. Suddenly, something comes into my dream, the Oracle.

He preaches, 'I have come again to guide you. Listen very carefully and remember, the map is in a museum in Dallas and you must not let it falls into Loki's hand. If it does, he will easily find out about Ghoul Lord's and if he does revive the Ghoul Lord, something terribly bad will happen.'

When he disappears, I wake up panting and sweating. Sarah also shocked when I wake up out of sudden. I embrace her and tell her that the map is in a museum. Sarah asks if we could have a look but I decline because we should be meeting Mr. Goddard. She suddenly remembers and nods at me. Together we go back to sleep and this time she holds me close in her arms.

Loki is busy finding information about the map. He knows actually that the map is in the museum. He has actually seen the map, the ancient scroll made of golden hemp that was drawn by a slayer who killed the Ghoul Lord to safe the village of Viking from his terror. The slayer was named Ivan Heimgar who was blessed by Heimdall to secure the village from the Ghoul Lord.

Looking at the flashback, "It is learnt that once the Ghoul Lord is a vassal to the Norse king. He is so greedy of land that he has become a tyrant to his serfs. He would kill anyone who refused to be conscripted and those who became the feudal army are as young as 16 and as old as 60. He claimed so many lands except the Hersirs—Hargor and Viktor. Both are equally powerful and influential. The Ghoul Lord who was that time Jarl Edward is so envy that both of them are praised by the king himself and he shed his hatred on them.

He prayed to Loki to obtain his trick so that both of them would be so unfortunate and lost their influence from the people and king. Thus, Loki heard him, appears in his dream and taught him the trick.

It is also coincident that Hargor and Viktor shared the same birthday. Edward then presented them the gifts for their birthday. Hargor was given a small chest of hundred African Rubies, the ancient Roman's treasure plundered from the Egyptians. Inside it, a possessed bat was hidden. It was taught by Loki as a bloodlust carrier. Whereas for Viktor, he presented two crates of golden hemps to him and the crates are carried by a Siberian husky chanted by Loki of the Evil Verses of Set (the Curse of Seth).

Hargor when opened up the chest was enchanted with the beauty of the rubies but suddenly, the bat freed and bit him. Time to time, he became enfeeble and finally, at night he thirst for blood and the symptom of Vampire plague happens. It is also said that this tale has the relationship with Vlad III of Romania.

Viktor in another case was a lord to Ivan Heimgar. Ivan was his favorite among the serfs. He served Viktor so well and he was the best soldier of Viktor's. There are legend said that Ivan got his blessing from Heimdall and that is the reason he owned the same strength as Heimdall. He had the courage, the power and the skill of war said to be possessed by Heimdall. Therefore, Viktor presented him some golden hemp as gift to sincerity.

As prophesied, Ivan was told that Viktor will be in trouble that the husky shall bite him and turn him into a Wolfman. Because both the Hersirs had changed immediately into the horrifying creatures killing the people thus they lost their influence from the people. Even the king had to hunt for them and Edward offered his help for him had avenged them.

Due to too keen of hunting them down, Edward had completely forgotten about his worship to Loki and Loki showed his wrath on him. He descend from the Valhalla, in a human form, he acquired the knowledge of voodoo from a trader to curse Edward to be a living dead. His spell wouldn't work if Edward isn't dead.

As Edward hunts for them, suddenly a foe of his, Ivan spotted him and shot an arrow to his back. He fell to the ground unconscious but still living. The curse is working and eating his mind and he was spelled into a Ghoul Lord in a few minutes always hunger for flesh.

First he would raid the tomb to consume the flesh but due to the taste, he started raiding the villagers and another time the king offered reward to anyone who could kill them. Eventually, Ivan could track him and defeated him by piercing an arrow given by Heimdall but the magic isn't strong enough to kill. The Ghoul Lord beheaded and his head was placed in an iron mask only to be displayed in the museum. It is believed that with the head, one could find the body too and after attaching both with a spell that the Ghoul Lord could be revived. And Ivan drew the map to his head only as guidance.

Unfortunately, he was slandered by someone he reported that he hid the head. He was killed and the map fell to the person's hand and he requested that he would be a navigator from Ghoul Lord. Ghoul Lord's head is said to fulfill any wish but if he revived, those who had asked for wishes will be turned into zombies. So the person's wish is fulfilled and he was with the Viking's crew founding the America. During the battle with the Indians, the map was dropped in the land of America which was found and bought to the museum.

There are only two methods of stopping the revival. First, is to stop Loki from finding the map or is to dispose the head in the sea. Never to attach with the body is the most important thing Sarah and I must do to prevent the revival. Otherwise, he cannot be stopped and the whole world will be doomed."

At 8 a.m. when the sun has risen, me and Sarah have our breakfast in a diner. She orders some pancakes and coffee and me, I order some sandwiches.

The worker smiles at us and asks me, 'An Aussie, are you?'

I nod our head and smile back at her.

I quickly ask, 'Do you know where the museum is?'

'Which museum exactly?'

'In Dallas I think.'

'It is in the downtown. I'm not so sure either because very seldom I go to the town.'

'Thank you, miss.'

Suddenly, Sarah caught a glimpse of Loki. He was seen walking among the crowd at a subway station. He is busy looking for the map but doesn't know where it is situated. He suspects that it should be in a government building maybe an archive or museum. When I ask Sarah why she was staring at the subway, she didn't answer.

Mr. Percy suddenly calls Sarah.

'Hello, Ms. Saunders? This is Percy speaking.'

'Hello Mr. Goddard, nice to hearing from you.'

'I am available at 1 p.m. and will that be a trouble to you?'

'I'm glad to be able to meet you on that time.'

'I believe meeting in the library would be good.'

'Sure, Mr. Goddard. And if I ask for goodwill, would you assist us by touring into the Alamo remembrance?'

'It would be a pleasure, Ms. Saunders. See you then. Good day.'

'Good day sir.'

She turns to me all radiant. Her face full with joy and exclaims, 'We have the source now!'

I hug her so gaily that we have found someone to help us in finishing our column. After the meal, Sarah points out that she needs some new and appropriate clothing for the meet in addition, she needs some new threads for casual.

I agree for I have to buy some too. So we spend our morning in the shopping mall and enjoying our day there. When afternoon comes, we change our clothes to meet Mr. Goddard. He was waiting at the guess room in the library when we arrived. He was reading the newspaper.

Sarah greets upon her arrival, 'Hi, Mr. Goddard and good afternoon. I am so sorry if we were late.'

'Hey, you must be Sarah and there's nothing to be sorry. This must be Alex Chrimson.'

I shake his hand, 'Pleasure to meet you, Mr. Goddard.'

'Yes, such a lovely day I will brief you about the Alamo and later we will have captions of the battle sites basically the San Antonio.'

'San Antonio would be far,' I utter.

'Quite far actually. Are you guys planning to go there?'

'If we have to.'

'You should. Actually it's a nice town.'

Then he goes explaining the Alamo, the revolution and the battles like the Battle of San Jacinto and who was in charged of the battle. He goes on narrating while explaining the pictures of the history and also the ups and downs during the war. We are so enthusiast with his speech which is so resourceful and also the reason behind the winning of Mexican in this battle.

We are quite astonished with the tales behind the cruelty of General Antonio Lòpez de Santa Anna and also the death of patriot especially Davy Crockett who was a famous icon on TV. First

I thought he is just a name of the show but after Mr. Goddard's explanation, I'm inspired. I'm quite appreciated with Mr. Goddard's time as he functions like a living Wikipedia.

After his briefing, we develop the first part and send a draft to our boss. We complete everything almost evening. The time is almost 3 p.m. so I suggest that we could have a look at the museum to see how the 'Golden Hemp' looks like. Sarah nods.

Outside the library, cabs are waiting in line for passengers. So easily one could catch a cab so do us. We are heading to the museum and the cabman just obeys. The museum is not quite far. Standing in the metropolitan so large and so beautiful the design is, and when we enter, it completely awes us.

There are a lot of items on display like fossils and many artifacts, scriptures, manuscripts and icons that describes the cultures, the tradition and the customs. I really like that place as it contains a lot of information, a lot of knowledge especially for students who are looking for resources. However, my motive is not for the tools but the map. We walk to the middle section where all the valuable artifacts are displayed such as portraits, jewelries from the Middle Ages, ceramics from Xia Dynasties and Middle East and many more and the most importantly, the map is in a glass display at one corner. Incredibly, Loki was there too hunches himself when staring at the thing.

We quickly haste to catch him but he is to fast to notice us and escape from the museum. Now that he had seen the thing and he would try however dangerous it is to get the map. I suggest that we talk to the management to double the security since the Loki will do whatever to steal the map.

Sarah stops me because it will be ridiculous to tell the management since we are not known to them. I fell into dilemma when she said that. All we have to do is to keep an eye always at the museum and just hoping that the guard will be very watchful on the thing.

At night, Loki plans to sneak in. He brings a bag of weapons with him. First, he drops a cell phone at the entrance knowing that nobody would find out. Then he climbs up to the top of the hotel block opposite the museum. The block is higher than the museum so he would have a perfect view of the museum. He prepares an anesthetic sniper aiming at the entrance of the museum. Then he waits until no passer by and he makes the call to the cell phone he dropped with another phone he has.

The phone rings quite a few times until a guard from inside the museum sensed the ringing, comes out and spotted a phone but when he picks up, Loki quickly hangs up. He aims at the guard and shoots the anesthetic which hits his shoulder. The guard then faints and Loki celebrates in his heart.

'Hopefully, this would last 6 hours,' he exclaims. Then, he shoots the grapnel from the gun which hit the rooftop of the museum and he glides down the rope like a flying fox. As he lands on there, he peeps through the roof which is made of glass and he could see two armed guards are below guarding the treasures. He throws in a canister of sleeping spore and when the canister breaks, the two guards are alarmed but so fast weakened as the spore spread so quickly. They fall to the ground snoring.

Loki then ties a rope around his waist and to the vent and jumps into the museum still restrain in the air. He never notices that there are security cameras surveying the area and so he falls into the surveillance notice. The personnel from the surveillance spotted someone is restraining on the air but trying to steal something so he quickly sounds the alarm.

Realized that he has been spotted, he quickly breaks the glass display with a hammer and grabs the map and he cuts off the rope. He quickly heads to the front door where only two guards are there. He throws the hammer at one of them but he ducks and the hammer missed and another one armed only with baton starting to chase him. He runs to the dinosaur prototype and hurls some bones at the guards. The bones missed and so the guards speed up to catch him. Knowing the entrance would be unlocked since the guard that guards the door has been anesthetized, he should escape easily provided there will be no cops yet.

The cops are chasing to the scene and this is witnessed by the Succubus and Felicia who were flying in the town. Then Loki appears running panicky in the street holding the Golden Hemp. The guards are chasing after him. The Succubus teleports to my room while Felicia finds Rowan after realizing something is wrong.

In my room, Succubus nudges us. We wake up annoyed but when it is the Succubus, there must be something wrong. She reports to us what she saw and we quickly storm to the ground floor. I need to find a car to chase to the scene so the Succubus quickly hijacks one of the parked cars unlocking it. I enter the car and activate the engine and immediately rush to the scene.

From a distance, we could hear the siren and so we follow the sound. Around the downtown, Loki is running hastily avoiding the guards and the cops. Rowan too is rushing together with Felicia but they hide at the rooftop of an apartment to remain unseen. It is been a dilemma whether to help out or not.

# EPISODE 13:
## THE FINALE OF THE GAME

Loki is running Rowan's way and Rowan filled with rampage wishes so much to kill him so Rowan jumps down from the roof right in front of Loki. Loki, who is stunned with Rowan's sudden appearance, tries to turn another way but Felicia is there too. So he has to storm into the apartment and climb all the way up the hallway to the roof. He should be very exhausted right now but due to desire to escape from the bars, he tries as hard as possible to reach the roof.

I park my car and quickly rush out and together, me and the monsters are chasing after Loki too. When he arrives at the rooftop, he quickly detaches the satellite dish and skates down the back alley staircase with it. When we finally arrive at the rooftop, the Loki guy has actually gone but we could hear the clanking sound at the back alley staircase. We rush there but he has actually gone together with the dish as protection.

Since Rowan has a great sense of smell, I request his help to track him. I call Sarah to drive to the back alley quick and as she arrives, I take her place and drive according to Rowan's guide in tracking the Loki.

Loki is running his way to the forest where he is heading to the plane. The map actually shows the location of Romania where the slain head is buried. I am quite surprise of the stamina the Loki guy has but we never know he would hijack a bike from a biker.

Therefore, Rowan stops at one place because he couldn't track anymore. Instead, he feels with instinct that Loki is heading to the woods. Base on his instinct, we ought to follow him into the forest. And in the forest, Loki's men have been very watchful. Three of them with shotguns are ready to fight us. One of them fires but hit Rowan and makes him enraged. Rowan leaps on him and scratches violently and he was left bleeding to death.

One of them terrified with that quickly loads two silver cartridges into the shotgun and fires at his shoulder and Rowan falls to the ground trembling and sweating. Seeing this, the Succubus and Felicia storm out and bash two of the guards. Two of them are thrown to the tree and left to dead too.

Rowan is suffering due to the breaking of the curse and slowly he turns to normal human. His fur started falling and his fangs become normal. His ears grow to a normal one that finally he changes to human. He is lucky because the ammo didn't hit kill him. He is just wounded and I ask Sarah to send him to the hospital quickly.

Now me, Succubus and Felicia should deal with Loki and return the map to the museum. Loki grabs a gun from his guard and points at Gerard's driver to force him to fly the plane. Meanwhile we are still tracking him in the jungle, Felicia smells of blood in the forest.

'I smell of blood,' she says.

'Me too and I believe they are around here,' Succubus agrees.

'Then, bring me to them and I hope this will be the last,' I emphasize.

We run into the woods and Loki is already in the plane. His only guard without arm charges at me but I knock him down unconsciously. The driver has already started the engine and the plane is about to fly so Felicia quickly teleports in.

Felicia teleports right to the back of Loki but the genius realized that, takes out a cross and points at Felicia. Felicia is shocked when she sees that cross and retreats whenever Loki approaches. Loki then opens up the emergency exit and forcing Felicia to exit with the cross. Felicia retreats and finally trip and fall from the exit.

The Succubus is astonished with Felicia's sudden teleportation to our location. She is panting and there is terror in her eyes.

'I have failed you, Mistress,' she apologizes to the Succubus.

'What was happening, Felicia?'

'He has a cross!'

'I know now. You teleport me inside and I would deal with him.'

Hearing this, the Succubus teleports me into the plane and quickly I knock Loki out. This time he fights back. He grabs his gun and hits me with the butt. He hits me at the abdomen and again at my back. So I retaliate by punching twice on his stomach and he accidentally fires a shot at the window.

Strong winds blow in and make the plane unstable. The driver notices that quickly covers the window pane with clothing and the Succubus lends her hand so he could resume operating the plane whereas me and Loki are still brawling. I have to kick his gun out of his reach and continue punching and bashing him.

It is very difficult to fight in the plane especially when it soars unstably in the air. It is very difficult to balance ourselves when we fight and at times when I almost defeat him, I would fall because of the gravity. Thus, remembering the words of Master Luo about water strider, I calm myself pretending that I'm just flying on the clouds. Loki suddenly charges out and spears me to the corner but I manage to recover and shove him away.

This time Loki could obtain his gun from the ground and points at me. The Succubus seeing this knocks him from his back and he was thrown to the emergency exit. I faster grab his map which is hanging on his belt. The Succubus reaches the emergency exit switch but I stop her. I know Loki must be brought to justice so I quickly grab a parachute bag and tie around him. I ask the Succubus to switch on the emergency exit and I instantly open up his parachute so he could be blown to the exit while restraining to the plane.

After that, I command the driver to fly back to Dallas. The driver obeys and we fly back to Dallas. The night is almost end when we finally land in the woods and when Felicia seeing us, rejoices and thanks me. The Succubus too is grateful with my quick thinking.

'I guess now, Lex that we have achieved what we should be doing so we must go back to our hometown.'

'You're welcome Felicia, Succubus. I guess the best way to go back is by plane. You can't teleport that far to Romania.'

'We actually have to since yeah, teleporting requires lot of energy. I am almost exhausted fighting with that guy.'

Then I turn to the driver, 'Could you just bring these chicks back home?'

The driver nods but quite in a frightening way. I smile and turn back to Felicia and Succubus.

'He hoped you wouldn't taste his blood.'

'We might just do that . . . being vegetarian,' Felicia laughs.

'You know Succubus doesn't eat nor sucks blood. That is just . . . yucks!' Succubus shows her expression.

I nod to them also laughing and before we separated, we shook our hands as symbol for friendship. This time I think no matter what people said about frightening monsters, it is just a matter of mindset and I appreciate their help.

Later the police car arrives and I turn to Loki.

'Loki, it is about time you face the justice.'

'You will pay for it, you effing maniac!'

'I guess I will genius. You see being so sly sometimes would harm so take my advice. To be clever, one not harms the others. So try not to be cunning. You will fall one day.'

Then the cops take him away. I return the 'Golden Hemp' to the officer but with caution.

'Sir, I would like to give you this but I suggest it should be destroyed. Otherwise, something bad would happen if someone has actually unveiled the secrets behind this map.'

'Ah. Comprender. But look here, son. The decision is not made by me. You should talk to the museum.'

'I agree, sir.'

Soon Sarah arrives. She hugs me tightly and when seeing me bruises, she slowly rubs and that is so soothing.

She asks, 'Are you alright?'

I nod, 'I guess I should. Thanks to master for his guidance.'

She smiles, 'How could you think of him in such a critical situation?'

'I didn't think of him. I see him.'

Sarah nods slowly and we both have a good laugh until suddenly Mr. Barry calls.

'Hello, boss.'

'Hello Alex. I want to say, you're both my prosperous employees. I would say the draft you sent me is great!'

'Of course sir. We have been working full time for that.'

'Ha-ha. Keep up the good work.'

'Aye, boss.'

Suddenly I realize. I ask Sarah about Rowan's condition.

'Don't worry. He just wounded his arm and he had those shells shrapnel removed. He is now stable and we can't see anymore Werewolves.'

'I hope he's alright. I wish to see him now.'

'Of course we will. Would you be driving there?'

'Sure.'

We drive to the hospital and Rowan is resting in Ward B. He is not asleep yet so I approach him.

'How do you feel now, Rowan?'

'Terrible.'

I'm surprised he said that.

Then he continues, 'Terrible as I disappoint you.'

'Like how exactly?'

'I have killed the innocence like Kat and Lita and lost such a beneficial friends like them. I'm feeling terribly sorry.'

'I know. We made mistakes but that has been a long time. Even Felicia and Succubus have forgiven you.'

Rowan breaks into tears and hugs me and Sarah and exclaims, 'I have found the best friends like both of you.'

'Eer, I guess ya. Thank you for that,' Sarah comforts him.

Later my phone rings again.

'Hello, Alex.'

'Hello and who is this?'

'I'm Gerard, the hotel manager. Remember?'

'Of course. How are you, Mr. Rosicky?'

'Just call me Gerard. I'm fine here and I would like to thank you profusely for finding my plane and catches the convicted.'

'Oh? Welcome sir. But how could the driver reaches Romania so quickly?'

'No he hasn't but he called.'

'Sorry. My foolishness. So how's the management in the hotel?'

'Splendid. Should you come back, I will charge you with discount. Good to hear from you again. Bye bye.'

'Goodbye.'

Sarah yawns again and Rowan thinks we should be back to the hotel. I agree with him so I together we drive back to the hotel.

The next morning the housekeeper knocks our door and I open. She hands me a newspaper and stare at me like so surprise and I wonder.

'Hel-lo. Thank you for the paper.'

'Did . . . did you assist . . . in . . . in capturing the . . . museum . . . thief?' she asks haltingly.

'Yeah why?'

'Nothing,' then she leaves.

This is such a weird morning. So I flip the newspaper and surprised with my face appeared in the newspaper. The headline 'Samaritans helping the cops capturing the museum thief' and I'm awed with that. Sarah too is stunned with the news.

'I guess I'm famous in the town, honey.'

'Yeah. I thought so.'

I remember that we still have two parts left for the column and I have a contact, Jan Ashbert. He is a Mexican mixed American and has been studied on the Alamo for several years. He would assist us as he has the artifacts from his great grandfather who had been siding General Antonio Lòpez Santa Anna. The appointment with him would be at 12 p.m. He is said to travel here from San Antonio and it would be a great source he would provide us.

The officer from the police station calls suddenly and I pick up.

'Hello, Mr. Chrimson?'

'Yes I am and you are . . . '

'I'm Officer Borrough. You met me when we caught this 'Loki' guy.'

'Yes. What happened to him?'

'He is still behind the bar but we need to talk to you.'

'I will be there sir.'

I drive to the police station where Officer Borrough has been waiting.

'This guy, do you know his real name?'

'He keeps claiming himself Loki. I don't know sir.'

'Would you tell me how did you met him?'

'I met him in Romania and he is after the map which believed could make the world a hotbed. That is why I try to stop him from stealing the map.'

'I don't quite understand but I see the point. I contacted the museum and they allow you to keep the map. Do whatever you like then but not to make Dallas a hotbed too.'

'Certainly sir.'

I am so happy with the decision the museum made and quickly retrieve the map but when I exit the museum, the Oracle was there.

'You have helped us well, Alex. I wish to have the map. So I would give instead.'

He shows me a medallion and continues, 'The medallion of tiger, one of the twelve zodiacs of the Chinese which means courage. Take this and keep an eye of it. You will be benefited by it.'

I pass him the map and he gives me the medallion and when I wear it, I feel a whole new strength in me. When he gets the map, he bows at me and disappears. I feel so cheerful after that that I have accomplished my mission.

Something speaks in my mind with Master Luo's voice, "Always when someone feels a little knowledgeable than others would show its pride. All of us born in this world would not be perfect, so be humble. Take tortoise as example, such a slow creature and we see this as weakness but in fact, it has been living more than 150 years and may attain lot of experiences. It may use its shell as protection to any hazard but still we see it as slow and useless and vulnerable to hazards. We are always wrong with that, so imperfect."

I just smile hearing that and appreciate such wisdom.